ARVIND GUPTA graduated from the Indian Institute of Technology, Kanpur (1975) with a degree in Electrical Engineering. He has written 15 books on science activities, translated 140 books into Hindi and presented 125 films on science activities on *Doordarshan.* His first book *Matchstick Models & Other Science Experiments* was translated into 12 Indian languages and sold over half a million copies. He has received several honours, including the inaugural *National Award for Science Popularization amongst Children* (1988), *Distinguished Alumnus Award of IIT, Kanpur* (2000), *Indira Gandhi Award for Science Popularisation* (2008) and the *Third World Academy of Science Award* (2010) for making science interesting for children. Currently he works at IUCAA's Children's Science Centre, Pune, and shares his passion for books and toys through his popular website http://arvindguptatoys.com

RESHMA BARVE studied Commercial Arts at the Abhinav Kala Mahavidyalaya, Pune. She is a freelance artist and designer and has illustrated many children's books.

This book was developed under a grant from the Navajibai Ratan Tata Trust.

Published by Scholastic India Pvt. Ltd.
A subsidiary of Scholastic Inc., New York, 10012 (USA).
Publishers since 1920, with international operations in Canada, Australia, New Zealand, the United Kingdom, India, and Hong Kong.

For information regarding permission, write to:
Scholastic India Pvt. Ltd.
A-27, Ground Floor, Bharti Sigma Centre
Infocity - 1, Sector 34, Gurgaon 122002 (India)

First edition: May 2013
Reprint: July; August 2013

ISBN-13: 978-93-5103-005-8

Printed at Shivam Offset Press, New Delhi

TOYS FROM TRASH

ARVIND GUPTA

ILLUSTRATIONS BY RESHMA BARVE

SCHOLASTIC

New York Toronto London Auckland
Sydney New Delhi Hong Kong

Contents

SAND SUCKS

1. FILL 3/4 BOTTLE WITH SAND.

2. ADD WATER UNTIL THE SAND IS SATURATED.

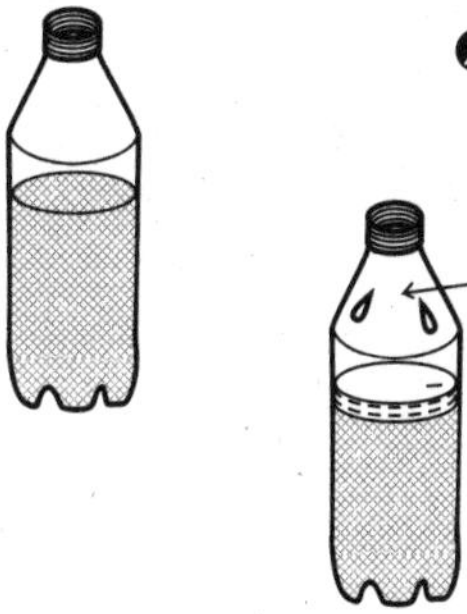

ADD SOME MORE WATER SO THAT A LITTLE FLOATS ON TOP.

3. ON PRESSING THE BOTTLE, MORE WATER SHOULD OOZE OUT FROM THE SAND. INSTEAD, THE EXTRA WATER IS SUCKED IN..

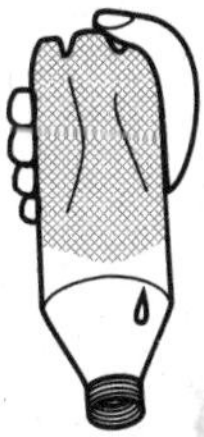

4. TURN THE PRESSED BOTTLE UPSIDE DOWN. SURPRISINGLY, NO WATER FALLS!

ON PRESSING, THE SAND STRUCTURE BREAKS CREATING INNER CAVITIES THAT SUCK IN THE EXTRA WATER.

EGG IN BOTTLE

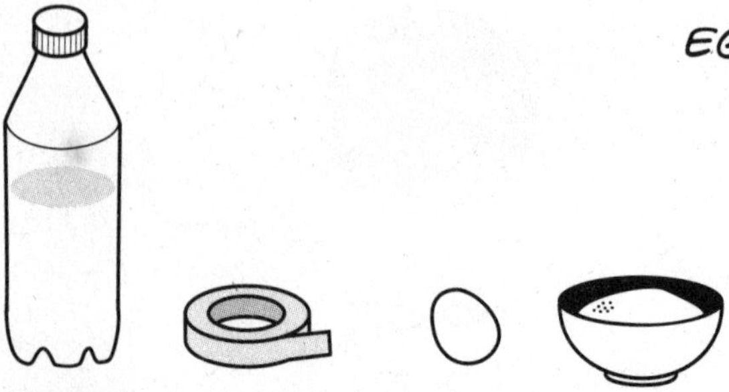

WATER BOTTLE

TAPE

EGG

SALT

❶ CUT BOTTLE 10 CM FROM TOP.

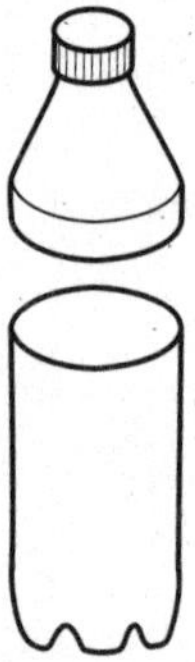

❷ FILL IT WITH TAP WATER.

❸ A FRESH EGG WILL SINK IN TAP WATER.

❹ ADD SALT AND KEEP STIRRING. ADD ENOUGH SALT SO THAT THE FRESH EGG FLOATS.

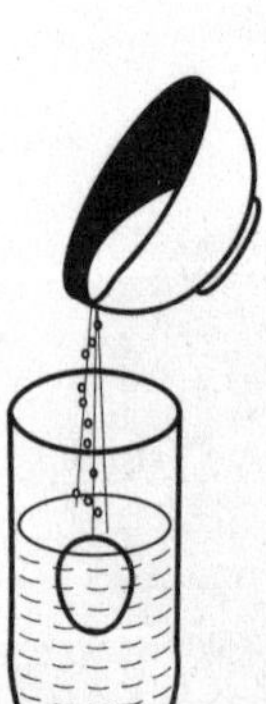

❺ ATTACH THE TOP PART OF THE BOTTLE WITH TAPE.

❻ NOW DROP BOTTLE FROM A HEIGHT OF SIX FEET.

THE EGG WILL NOT BREAK BECAUSE IT FLOATS IN A FLUID WITH THE SAME DENSITY—LIKE A BABY IN A MOM'S BELLY

REPEAT THIS EXPERIMENT WITHOUT SALT AND THE EGG WILL BREAK.

CANDLE SEE – SAW

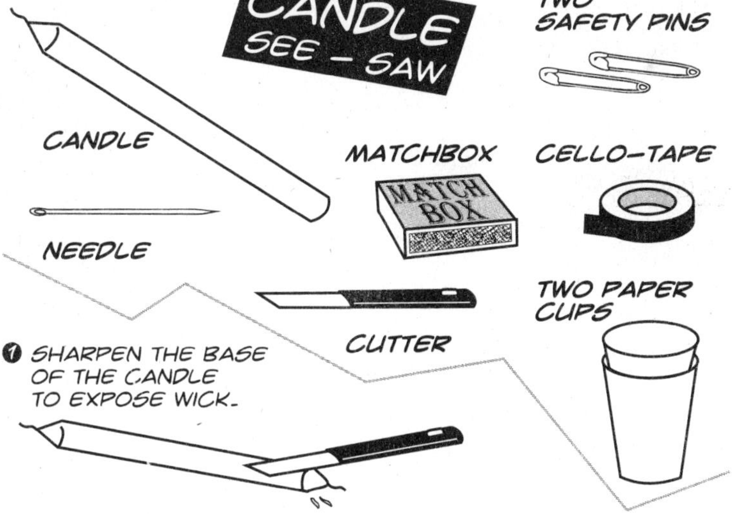

1. SHARPEN THE BASE OF THE CANDLE TO EXPOSE WICK.

2. POKE A NEEDLE THROUGH THE MIDDLE OF THE CANDLE.

THE CANDLE SHOULD BE EQUALLY BALANCED ON BOTH SIDES OF THE NEEDLE.

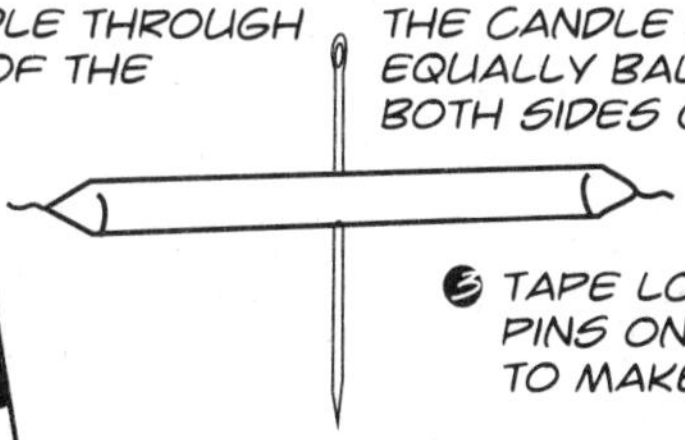

3. TAPE LONG SAFETY PINS ON TWO CUPS TO MAKE A STAND.

4. PLACE THE ENDS OF THE NEEDLE IN THE EYES OF THE PINS.

5. LIGHT CANDLE AT BOTH ENDS.

AS WAX DROPS FROM BOTH ENDS OF THE CANDLE, ITS WEIGHT WILL SHIFT AND A SEE–SAW MOTION WILL SET IN.

ATOMIC ARRAY

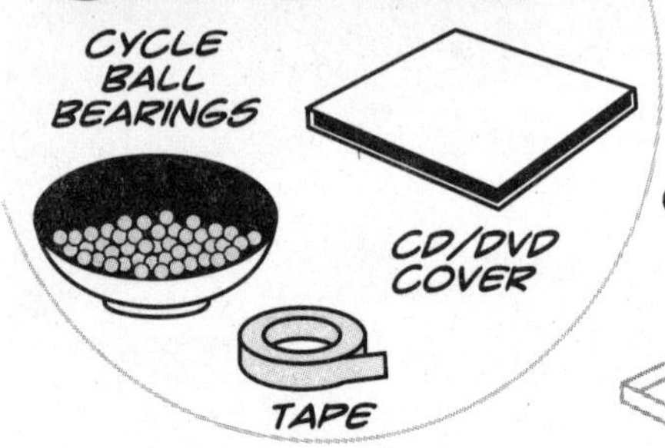

1. OPEN THE CD COVER AND REMOVE THE CD HOLDER.

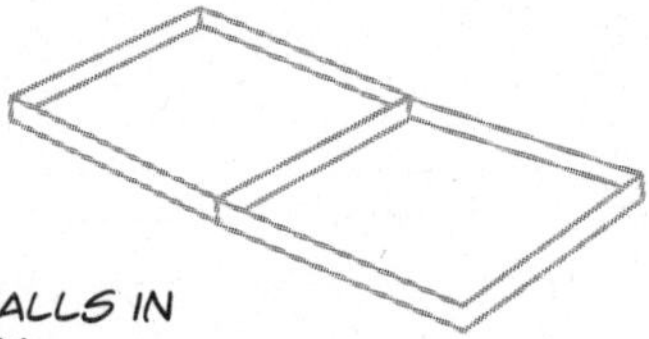

2. PLACE LOTS OF BALLS IN THE EMPTY CD BOX.

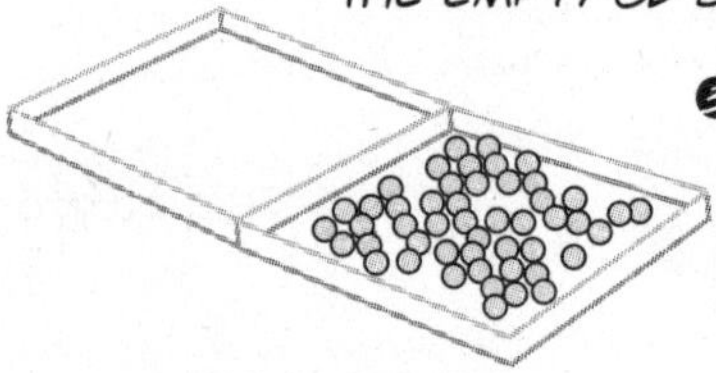

3. SEAL JOINTS WITH TAPE. SHAKE THE BOX AND OBSERVE THE RANDOM BROWNIAN MOTION OF THE STEEL BALLS.

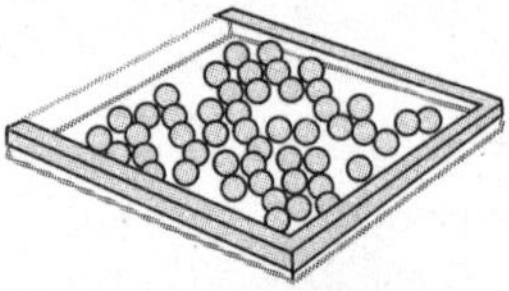

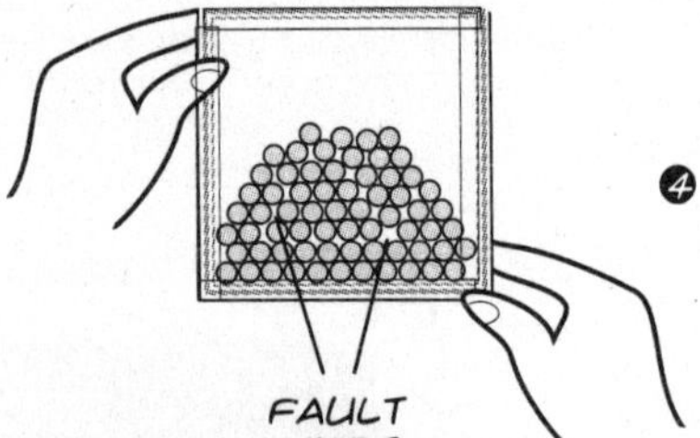

4. SHAKE AND OBSERVE CLOSE PACKING AND FAULT LINES AS IN AN ATOMIC ARRAY.

SEE CLOSE PACKING OF ATOMS.

MATTER IS COMPOSED OF ATOMS PACKED TOGETHER IN A LATTICE. AT PLACES THERE ARE GAPS AND FAULT LINES.

ADD SUGAR BEND LIGHT

1. ADD A FEW DROPS OF ANTISEPTIC LIQUID TO WATER. THE ANTISEPTIC HELPS IN ILLUMINATING THE PATH OF LIGHT.

2. ADD 500 GMS SUGAR TO WATER.

ATTENTION: DO NOT STIR AT ALL FOR 24 HOURS.

AFTER 24 HOURS, THE SUGAR WILL DISSOLVE IN WATER AND THE WATER WILL APPEAR CLEAR. HOWEVER, THE WATER WILL BE MORE DENSE AT THE BOTTOM AND LESS DENSE AT THE TOP. THERE WILL BE A DENSITY GRADIENT.

3. ON SHINING LASER ON TOP, THE BEAM WILL GO STRAIGHT.

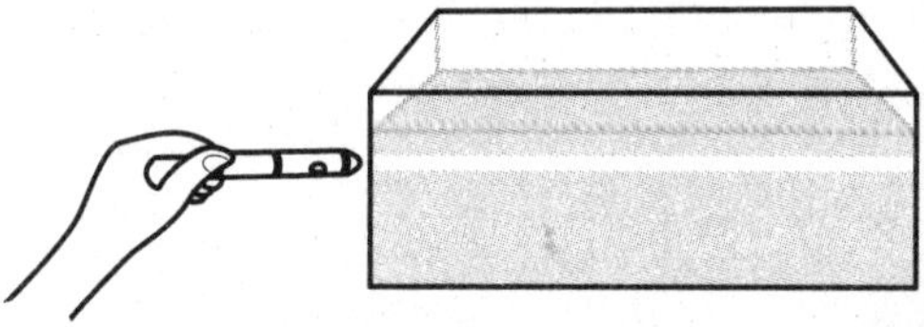

THE BEAM BENDS BECAUSE OF THE DENSITY GRADIENT IN THE SUGAR SOLUTION.

AS YOU GO LOWER DOWN, THE LASER BEAM WILL BEND.

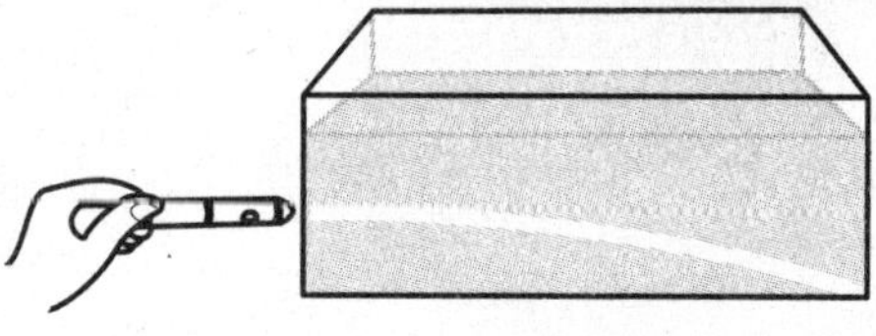

COLOURED CHROMA

❶ MAKE A HOLE IN THE MIDDLE OF THE FILTER PAPER.

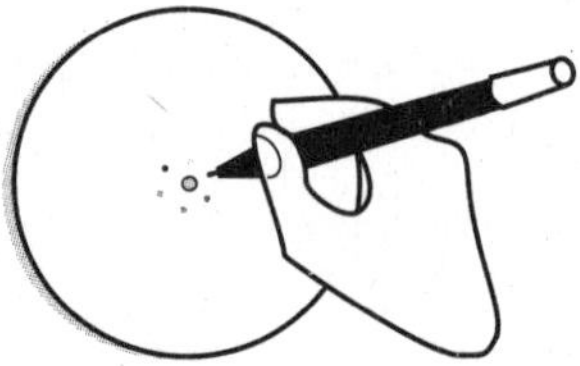

❷ DRAW DIFFERENT COLOURED DOTS AROUND THE HOLE.

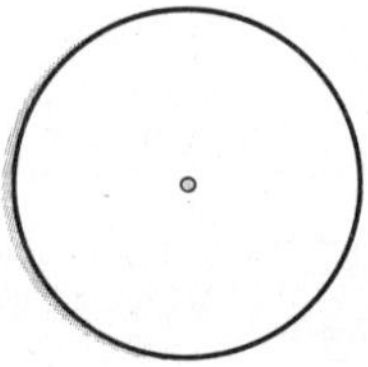

❸ MAKE A CONICAL BEAK FROM THE TOILET PAPER.

❹ INSERT THE CONE IN THE FILTER PAPER.

❺ PLACE THE FILTER PAPER ON A GLASS FILLED WITH WATER. THE BASE OF THE CONE MUST BE IMMERSED IN WATER.

AFTER A WHILE A BEAUTIFUL PATTERN WILL EMERGE.

MAKE YOUR OWN PICTURE PATTERN CARDS.

AS A RESULT OF CHROMATOGRAPHY VARIOUS COLOURS TRAVEL AT DIFFERENT SPEEDS AND SEPARATE OUT.

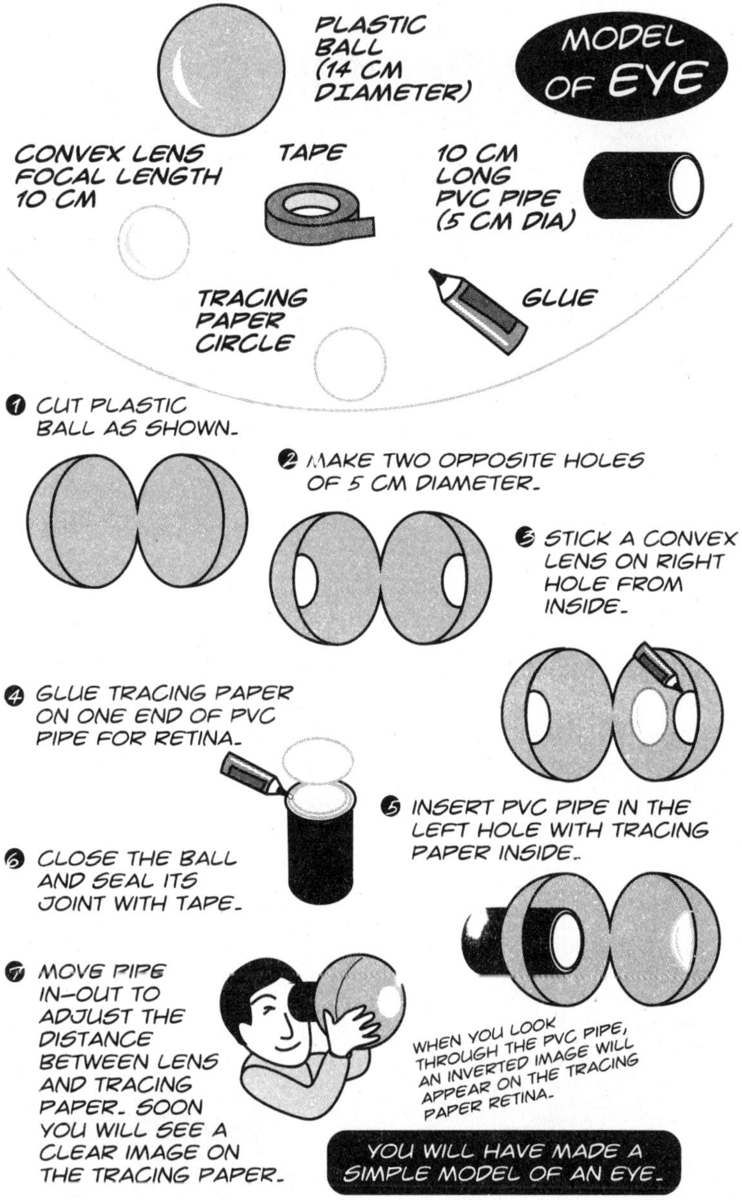
MODEL OF EYE
PLASTIC BALL (14 CM DIAMETER)
CONVEX LENS FOCAL LENGTH 10 CM
TAPE
10 CM LONG PVC PIPE (5 CM DIA)
TRACING PAPER CIRCLE
GLUE
1 CUT PLASTIC BALL AS SHOWN.
2 MAKE TWO OPPOSITE HOLES OF 5 CM DIAMETER.
3 STICK A CONVEX LENS ON RIGHT HOLE FROM INSIDE.
4 GLUE TRACING PAPER ON ONE END OF PVC PIPE FOR RETINA.
5 INSERT PVC PIPE IN THE LEFT HOLE WITH TRACING PAPER INSIDE.
6 CLOSE THE BALL AND SEAL ITS JOINT WITH TAPE.
7 MOVE PIPE IN–OUT TO ADJUST THE DISTANCE BETWEEN LENS AND TRACING PAPER. SOON YOU WILL SEE A CLEAR IMAGE ON THE TRACING PAPER.
WHEN YOU LOOK THROUGH THE PVC PIPE, AN INVERTED IMAGE WILL APPEAR ON THE TRACING PAPER RETINA.
YOU WILL HAVE MADE A SIMPLE MODEL OF AN EYE.

CAPILLARY ACTION

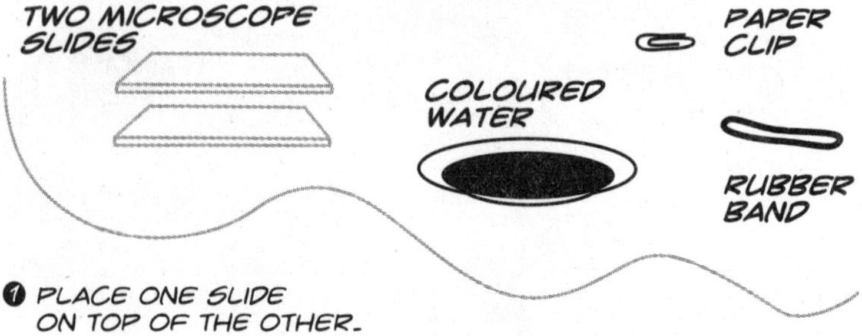

1. PLACE ONE SLIDE ON TOP OF THE OTHER.

2. INSERT A PAPER CLIP BETWEEN THE SLIDES AT ONE END. PLACE A RUBBER BAND ON THE OTHER END.

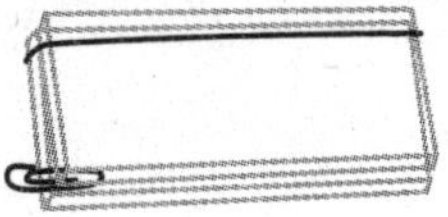

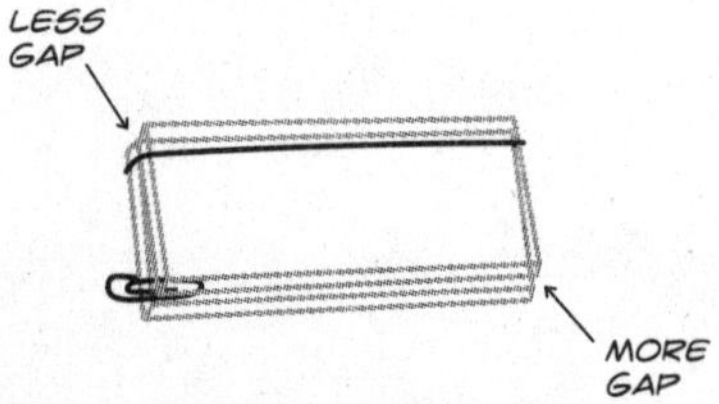

3. PLACE THE SLIDES VERTICALLY IN COLOURED WATER.

BECAUSE OF SURFACE TENSION, THE COLOURED WATER WILL RISE IN A BEAUTIFUL PARABOLIC CURVE.

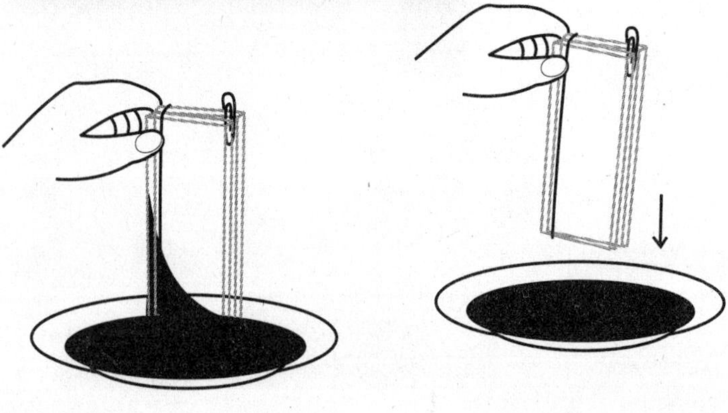

SOLID LIQUID

2 PARTS CORN FLOUR

1 PART WATER

BIG BOWL

❶ MIX 2 PARTS OF CORN FLOUR WITH ONE PART OF WATER.

CORN FLOUR + WATER MAKES A VERY GOOD SLURRY.

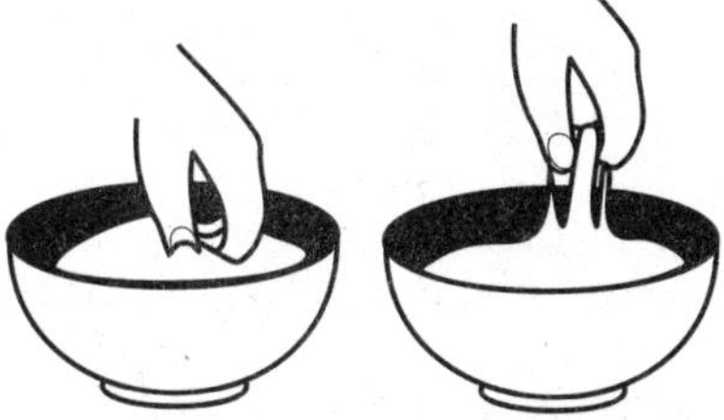

❷ SLOWLY DIP YOUR FINGERS IN THE SLURRY. YOUR FINGERS WILL GO IN QUITE EASILY.

❸ NOW PUNCH HARD ON THE SURFACE OF THE SLURRY. YOU WILL ENCOUNTER A SOFT WALL. YOUR FIST WILL NOT GET WET.

CORN PARTICLES COME TOGETHER AS YOU PUNCH HARD. THIS MAKES THE SLURRY SOLID.

THE SURFACE OF THE SLURRY ACTS LIKE A SOFT WALL.

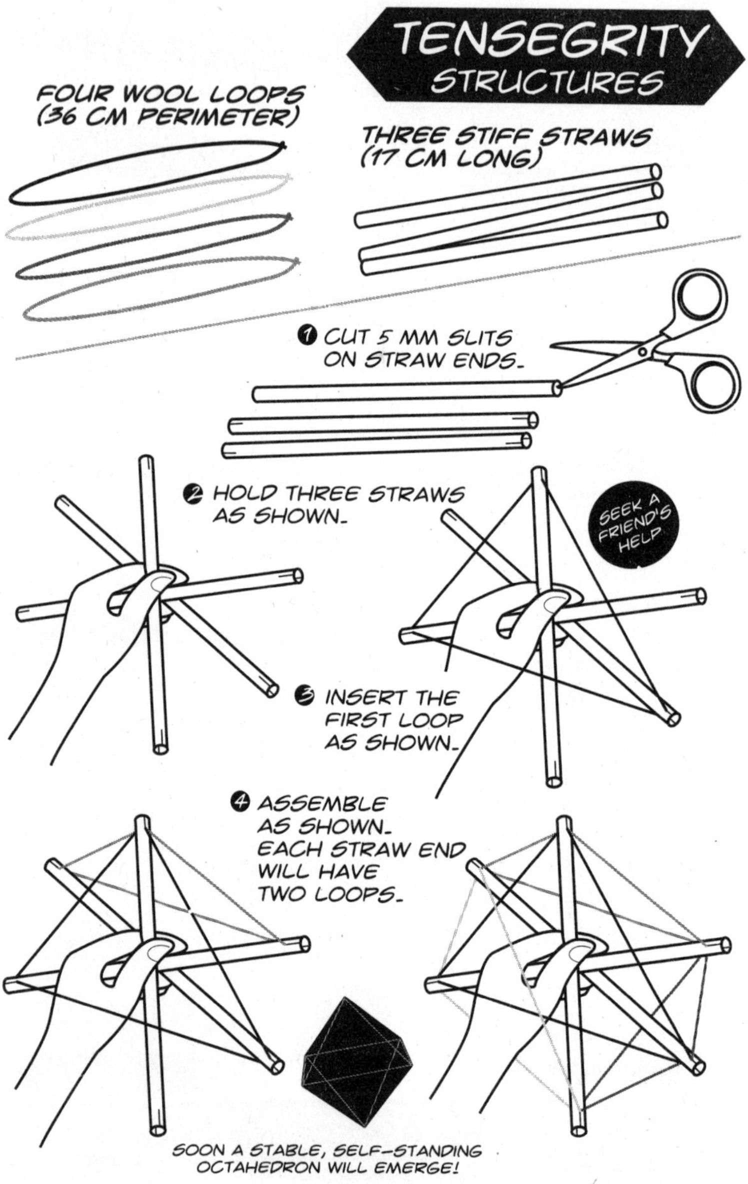
TENSEGRITY STRUCTURES
FOUR WOOL LOOPS (36 CM PERIMETER)
THREE STIFF STRAWS (17 CM LONG)
1 CUT 5 MM SLITS ON STRAW ENDS.
2 HOLD THREE STRAWS AS SHOWN.
SEEK A FRIEND'S HELP
3 INSERT THE FIRST LOOP AS SHOWN.
4 ASSEMBLE AS SHOWN. EACH STRAW END WILL HAVE TWO LOOPS.
SOON A STABLE, SELF-STANDING OCTAHEDRON WILL EMERGE!

MAKE ANOTHER STRUCTURE

SIX WOOL LOOPS
(35 CM PERIMETER)

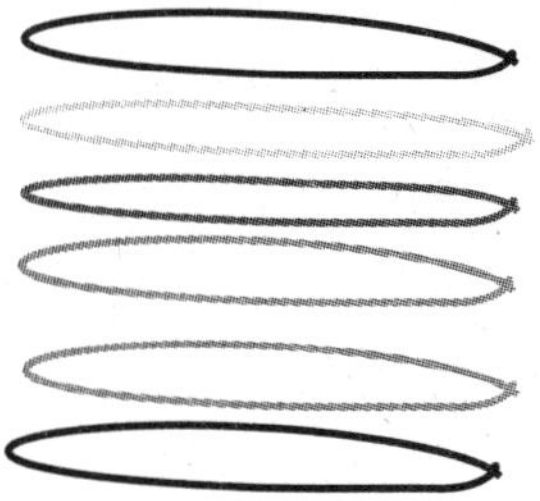

SIX STIFF STRAWS
(15 CM LONG) WITH
5 MM SLITS ON ENDS

❶ INSERT WOOL LOOPS
IN THE NOTCHES OF
ALL SIX STIFF STRAWS
AS SHOWN.

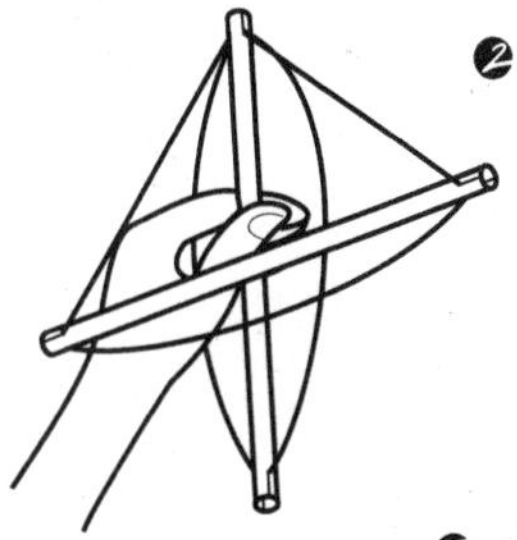

❷ ASSEMBLE
AS SHOWN.

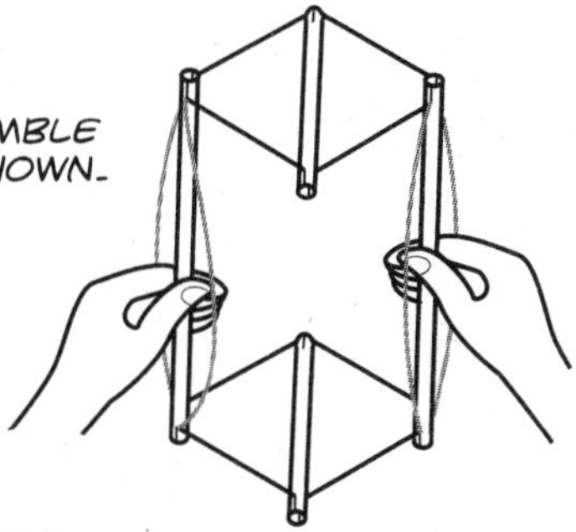

❸ ASK FOR A
FRIEND'S
HELP TO
ASSEMBLE.

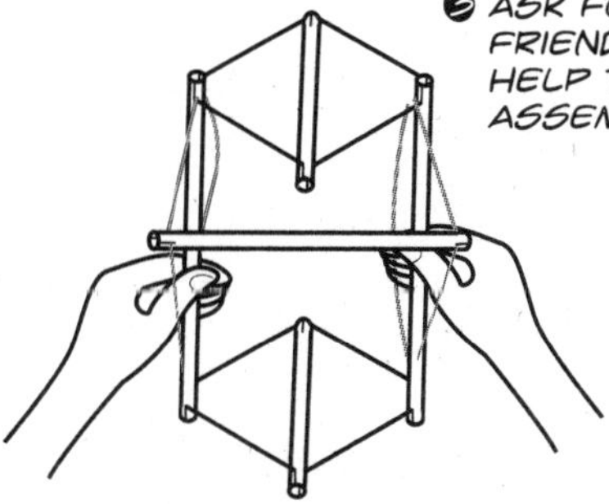

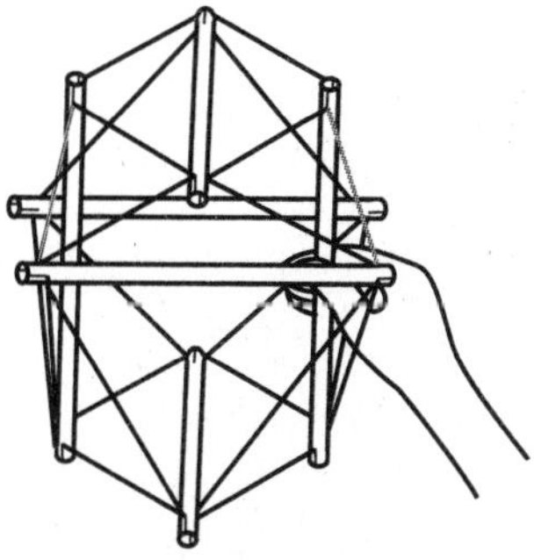

ALL THE STRAWS WILL BE UNDER COMPRESSION AND THE WOOL LOOPS WILL BE IN TENSION. SOON A STABLE AND ELEGANT STRUCTURE WILL EMERGE.

DOLL ON ROPE

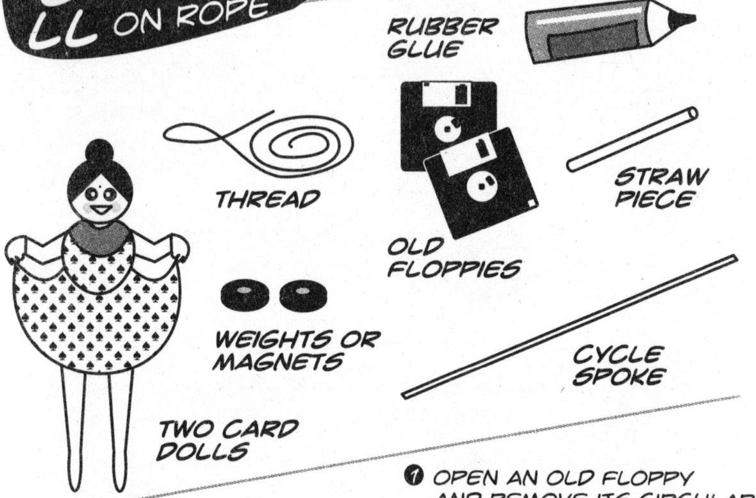

1. OPEN AN OLD FLOPPY AND REMOVE ITS CIRCULAR FILM. ALSO REMOVE TWO METAL DISCS.

2. STICK TWO DISCS BACK-TO-BACK TO MAKE A PULLEY. INSERT A STIFF STRAW OR REFILL AS BEARING.

3. INSERT PULLEY IN CYCLE SPOKE AND THEN BEND IT INTO A 'U' SHAPE.

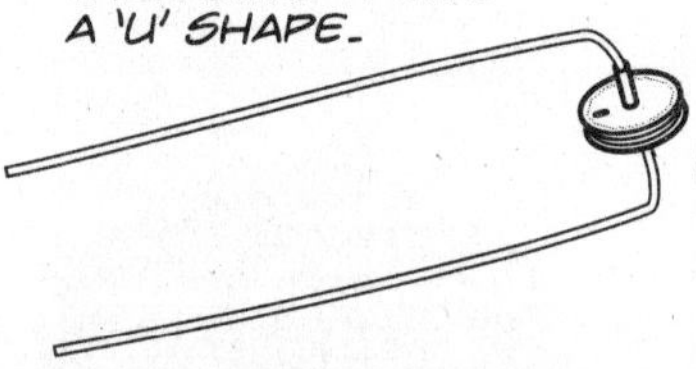

4. DRAW AND CUT THE FRONT AND BACK OF A CARD DOLL.

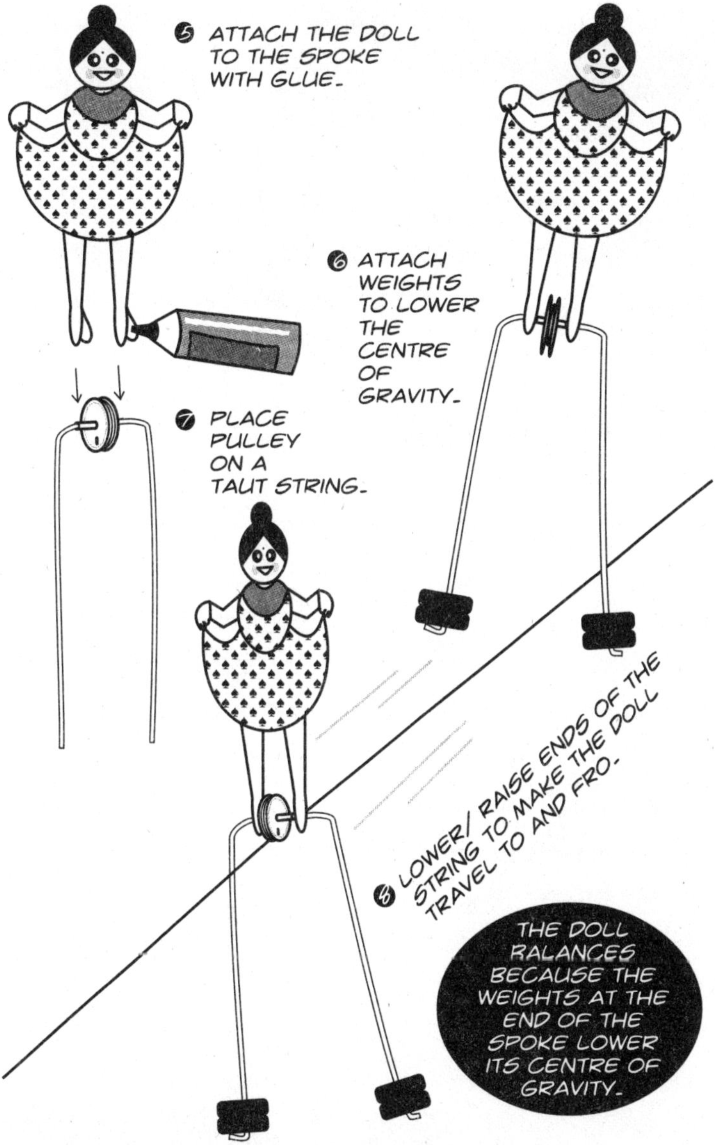
5 ATTACH THE DOLL TO THE SPOKE WITH GLUE.
6 ATTACH WEIGHTS TO LOWER THE CENTRE OF GRAVITY.
7 PLACE PULLEY ON A TAUT STRING.
8 LOWER/ RAISE ENDS OF THE STRING TO MAKE THE DOLL TRAVEL TO AND FRO.
THE DOLL BALANCES BECAUSE THE WEIGHTS AT THE END OF THE SPOKE LOWER ITS CENTRE OF GRAVITY.

STICK MAN

1. CUT ICE-CREAM STICKS WITH A CUTTER AND GLUE THEM TO MAKE A STRUCTURE AS SHOWN.

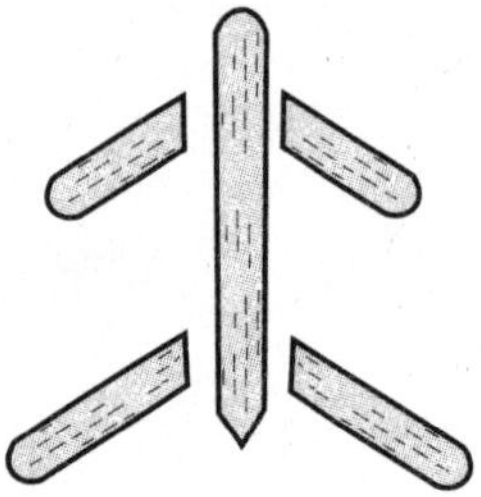

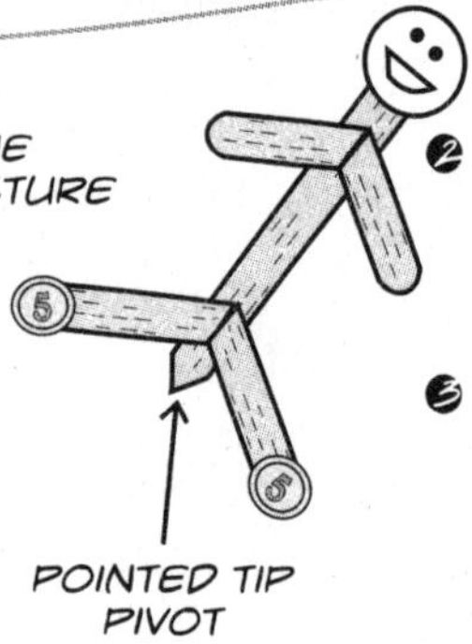

2. STICK A BOTTLE CAP AS HEAD. THEN DRAW A FACE.

3. STICK COINS ON FEET TO LOWER THE CENTRE OF GRAVITY.

4. PLACE THE POINTED TIP OF THE STICK MAN ON THE LID OF A HEAVY BOTTLE FILLED WITH SAND.

5. THE TOY WILL BALANCE ITSELF WITHOUT FALLING. PUSH IT A LITTLE AND IT WILL ROCK AND SPIN AROUND.

YOU CAN ALSO BALANCE IT ON YOUR FINGER TIP.

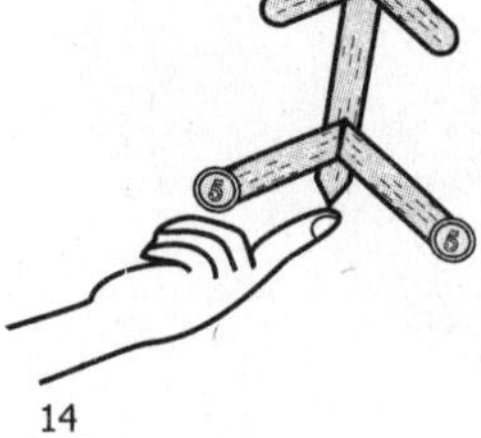

THE HEAVY COINS LOWER THE CENTRE OF GRAVITY AND THIS HELPS THE STICK MAN TO BALANCE.

COOL BOTTLE

1. WRAP FOIL ON A 1-L BOTTLE.

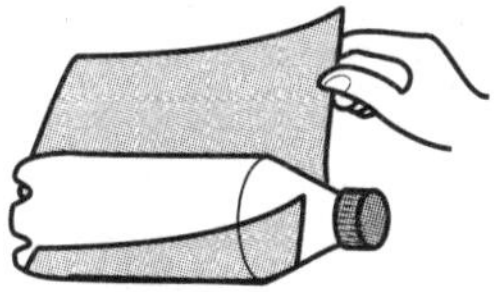

2. THEN WRAP IT IN SIX LAYERS OF NEWSPAPER FOR INSULATION.

3. CUT A 1.5 LITRE BOTTLE AS SHOWN.

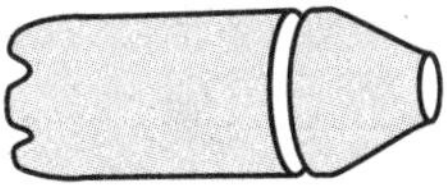

4. PLACE THE 1 LITRE BOTTLE IN THE BIG BOTTLE.

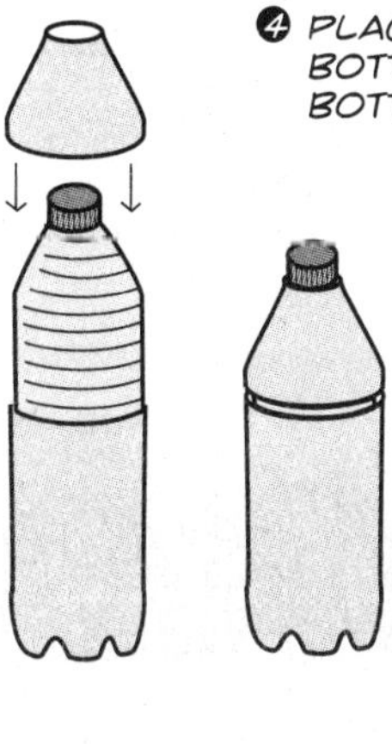

5. JOIN THE TWO HALVES OF THE BIG BOTTLE WITH TAPE. ATTACH A STRING TO COMPLETE THE THERMOS.

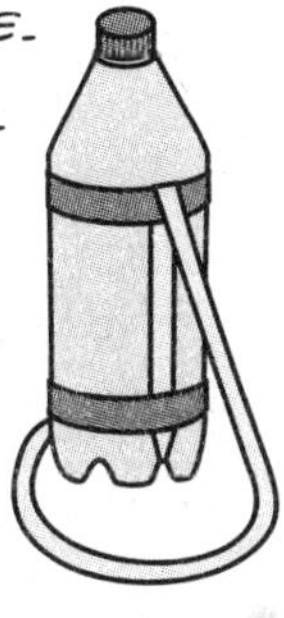

THE FOIL REFLECTOR AND NEWSPAPER INSULATION KEEPS THE WATER IN THE THERMOS COOL FOR A FEW HOURS.

ANNEALING IN ACTION

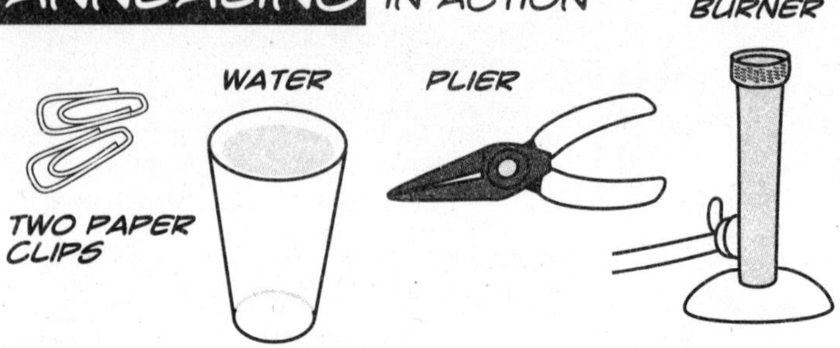

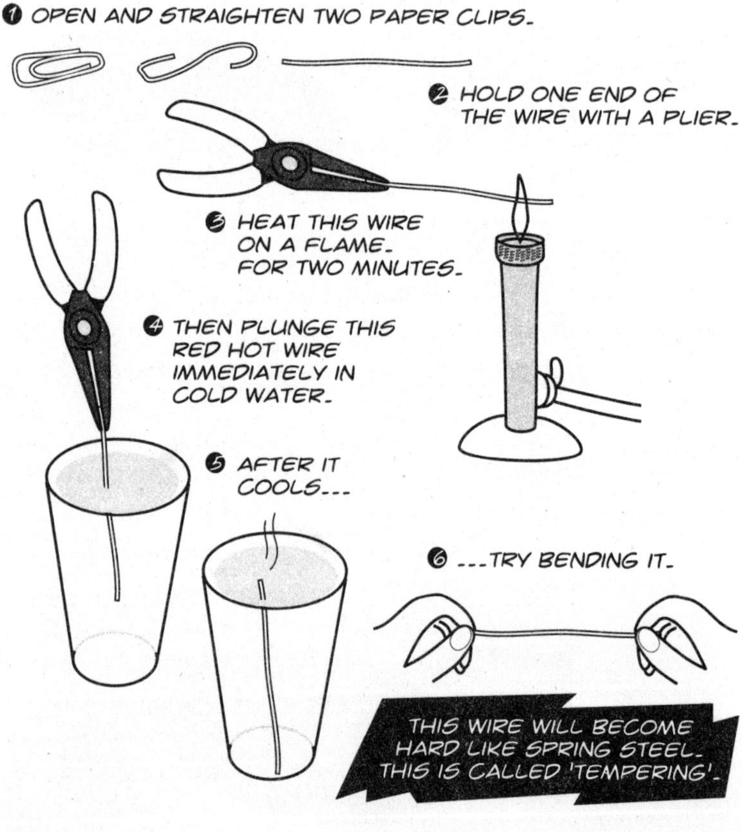

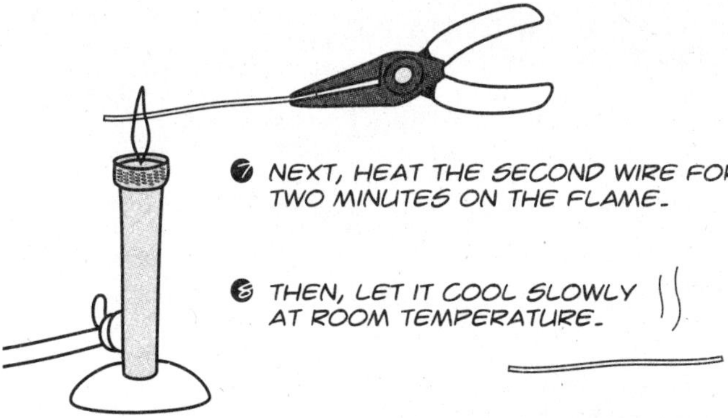

7. NEXT, HEAT THE SECOND WIRE FOR TWO MINUTES ON THE FLAME.

8. THEN, LET IT COOL SLOWLY AT ROOM TEMPERATURE.

9. BEND IT.

MINI SOLAR HEATER

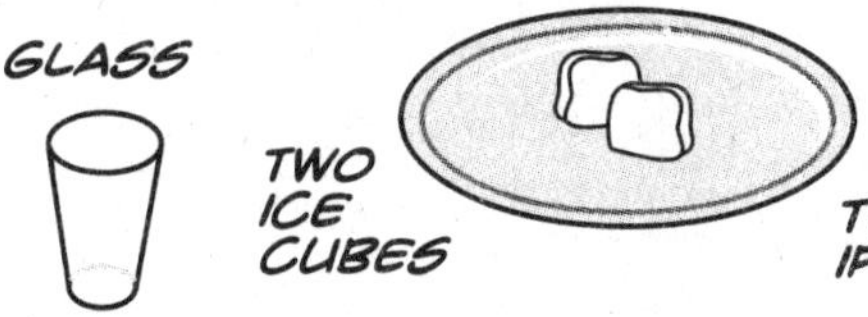

1. PLACE TWO SAME-SIZED ICE CUBES ON TWO PLATES AND KEEP THEM IN THE SUN.

2. COVER ONE CUBE WITH A TRANSPARENT GLASS.

YOU WILL OBSERVE THAT THE COVERED CUBE WILL MELT MORE.

THE GLASS ACTS LIKE A MINI SOLAR COOKER.

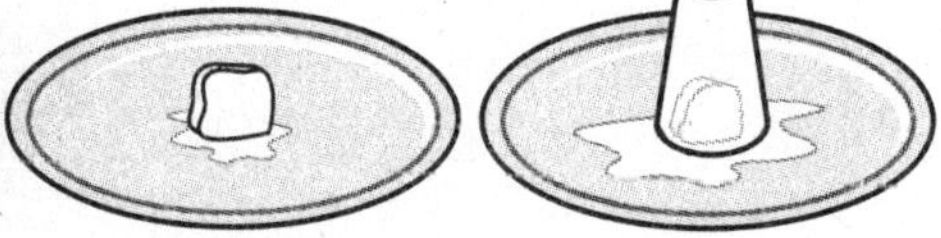

PEARL ON HOT PAN

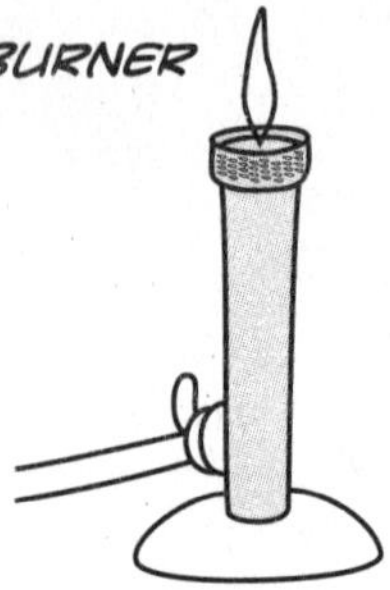

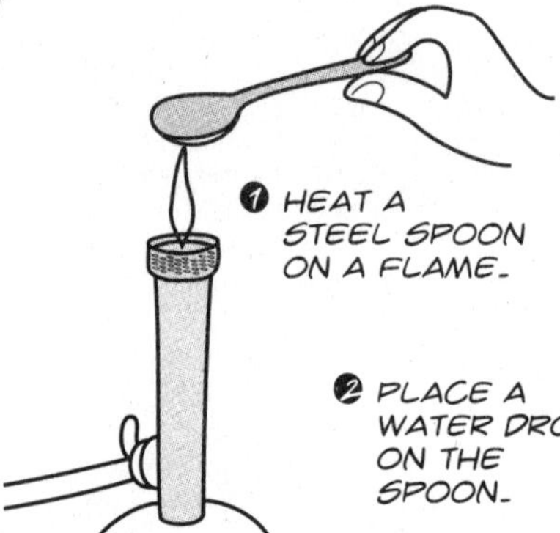

1. HEAT A STEEL SPOON ON A FLAME.

2. PLACE A WATER DROP ON THE SPOON.

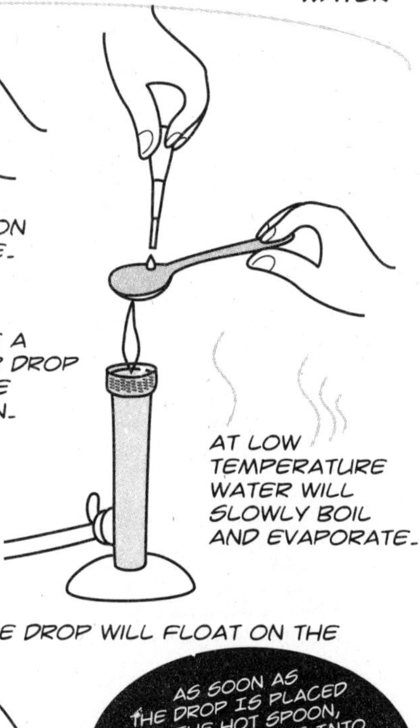

3. NOW HEAT THE SPOON A LITTLE MORE AND THEN PLACE ANOTHER DROP.

AT LOW TEMPERATURE WATER WILL SLOWLY BOIL AND EVAPORATE.

AT HIGH TEMPERATURE THE DROP WILL FLOAT ON THE SPOON LIKE A PEARL.

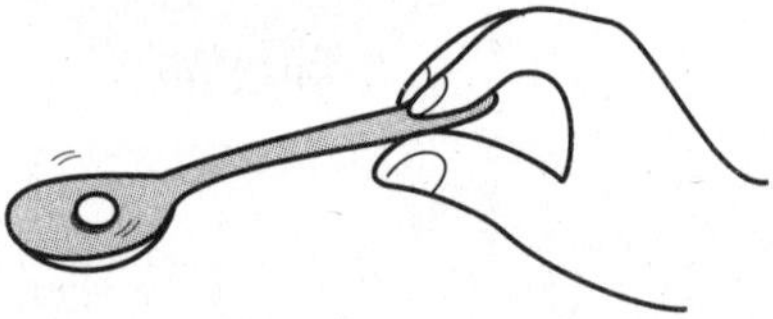

AS SOON AS THE DROP IS PLACED ON THE HOT SPOON, PART OF IT TURNS INTO VAPOUR. THIS FORMS AN INSULATING LAYER AND ENABLES THE DROP TO FLOAT LIKE A BEAD.

EXPANSION OF AIR

❶ WET A COIN...

❷ ...AND PLACE IT ON THE MOUTH OF A GLASS BOTTLE.

❸ RUB YOUR PALMS TO WARM THEM AND PRESS THEM ON THE BOTTLE.

❹ AFTER A WHILE THE AIR INSIDE WILL EXPAND AND THE COIN WILL RISE AND FALL WITH A PUCK SOUND.

THIS SIMPLE EXPERIMENT SHOWS THAT AIR EXPANDS ON HEATING.

SPOON PROPELLER

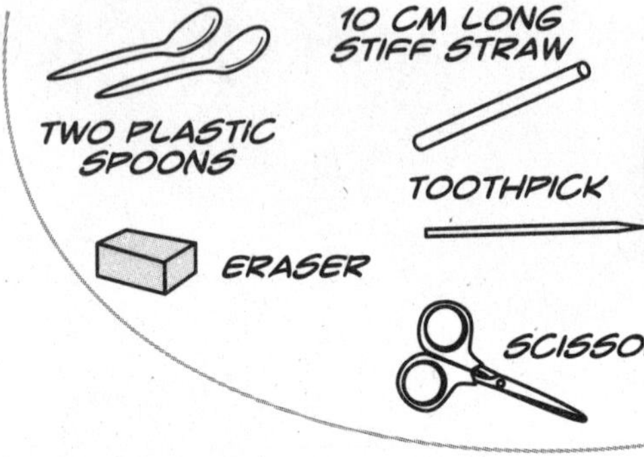

1. MAKE HOLES IN AN ERASER.

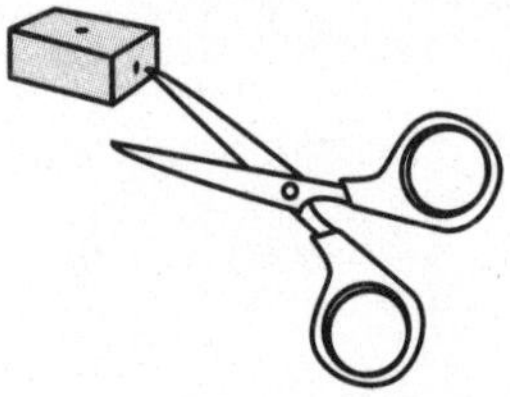

2. INSERT SPOONS IN THE ERASER. THEY SHOULD BE INCLINED IN OPPOSITE DIRECTIONS.

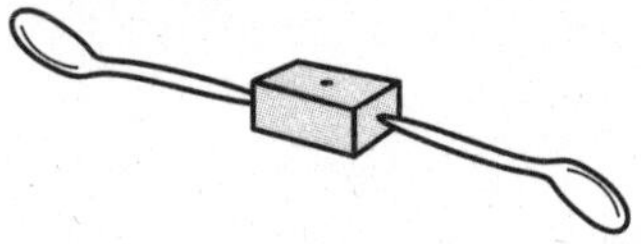

3. INSERT A TOOTHPICK IN THE ERASER AS SHOWN.

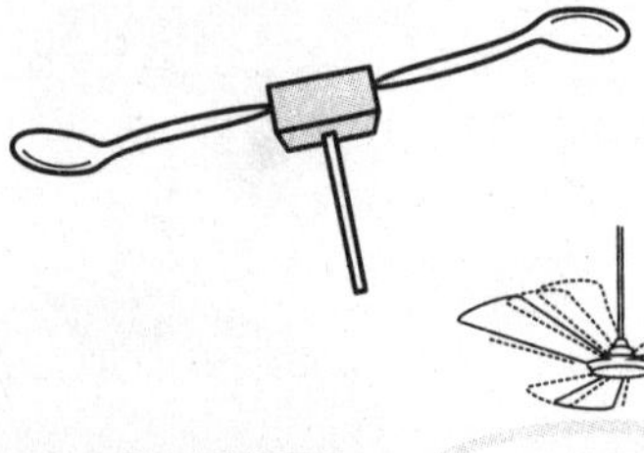

4. PLACE THE TOOTHPICK IN A STIFF AND LOOSE STRAW.

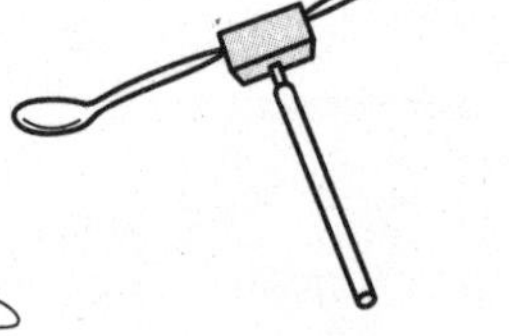

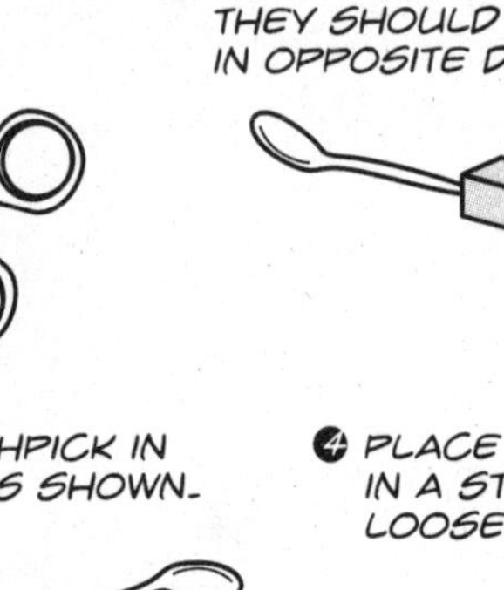

5. PLACE UNDER A CEILING FAN TO MAKE THE SPOON PROPELLER SPIN.

AIR FROM THE CEILING FAN STRIKES THE SPOONS AT AN ANGLE AND MAKES THEM SPIN.

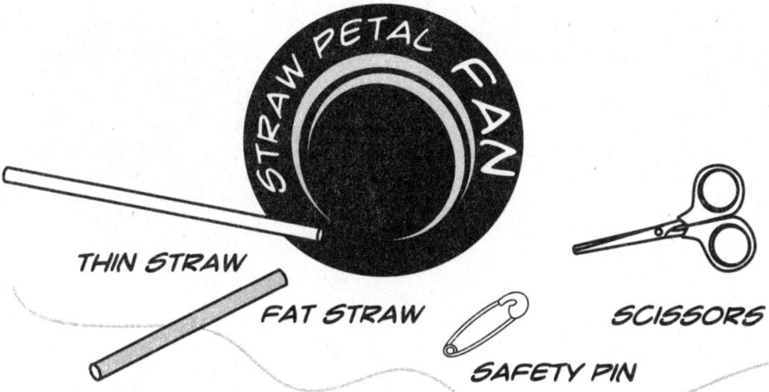

1. CUT FOUR, 5-CM LONG PETALS IN A FAT STRAW.

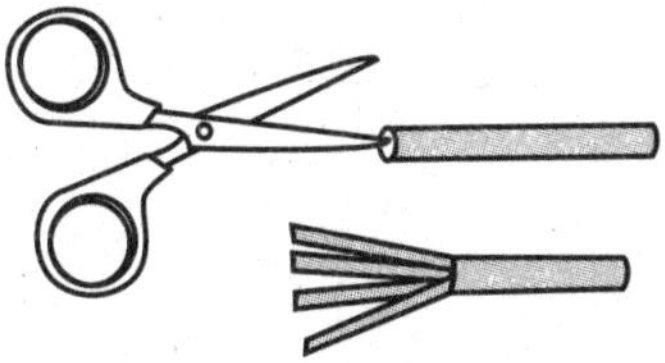

2. TWIST THE PETALS TO MAKE FAN BLADES.

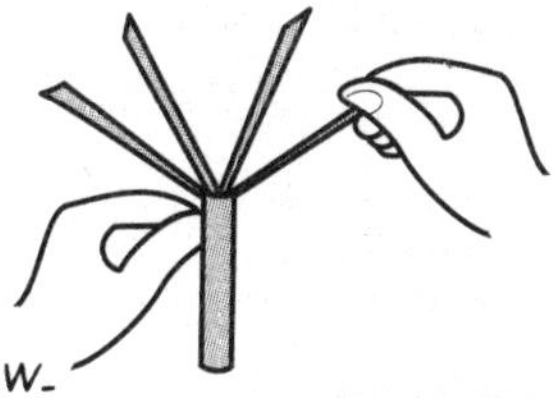

3. FIX A SAFETY PIN IN A THIN STRAW. THE PIN WILL PREVENT THE FAN FROM FALLING.

4. PLACE THE STRAW PETAL FAN IN THE THIN STRAW.

5. BLOW TO MAKE IT SPIN.

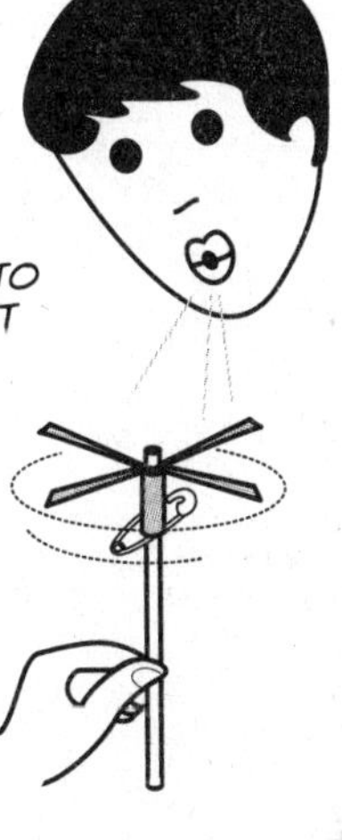

AS YOU BLOW, AIR STRIKES THE STRAW PETALS AT AN ANGLE AND MAKES THE FAN SPIN.

WATER TURBINE

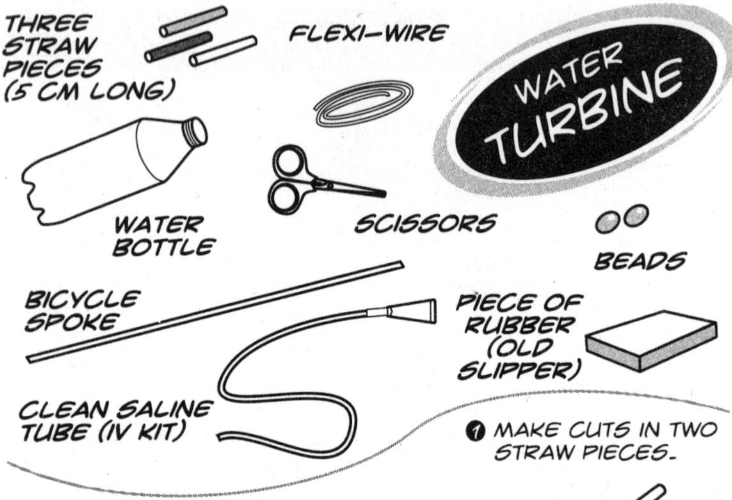

1. MAKE CUTS IN TWO STRAW PIECES.

2. MAKE A SIX BLADE TURBINE USING THREE PIECES OF STRAW AS SHOWN. MAKE A HOLE IN THE CENTRE OF THE STAR TURBINE TO INSERT THE "U" SHAPED WIRE AXLE. PLACE BEADS ON BOTH ENDS OF THE WIRE AS STOPPERS.

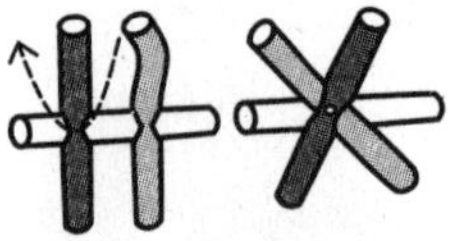

3. MAKE A STAND BY INSERTING A CYCLE SPOKE IN A RUBBER BASE.

4. DIP ONE END OF SALINE TUBE IN A WATER BOTTLE KEPT HIGH UP.

5. FIX THE OTHER END OF THE SALINE TUBE IN THE RUBBER HOLE.

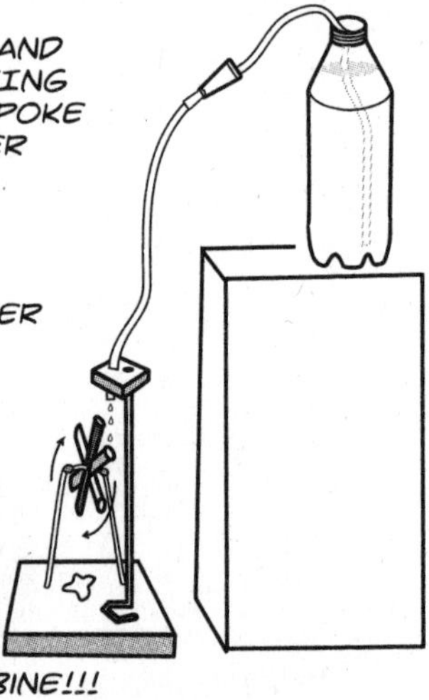

THE DRIPPING WATER FROM THE SALINE TUBE WILL ROTATE THE TURBINE!!!

ANIMATION ON FLYWHEEL

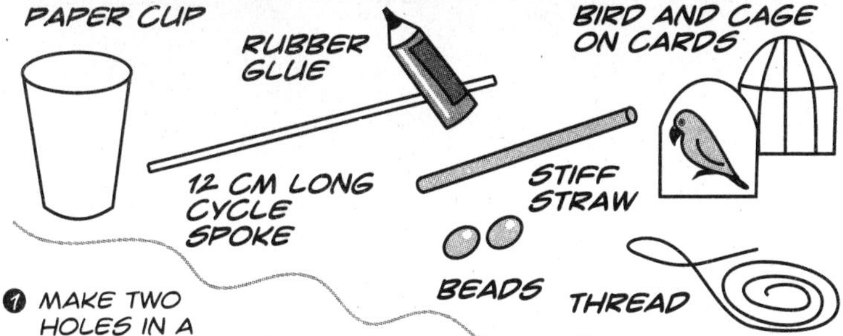

1. MAKE TWO HOLES IN A PAPER CUP.

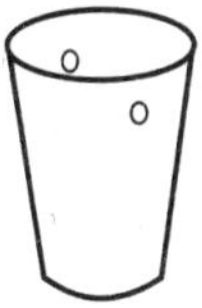

2. WEAVE A STIFF STRAW THROUGH THE HOLES AND FIX IT WITH RUBBER GLUE.

3. STICK PARROT AND CAGE BACK-TO-BACK ON A CYCLE SPOKE. WEAVE A BEAD IN THE SPOKE.

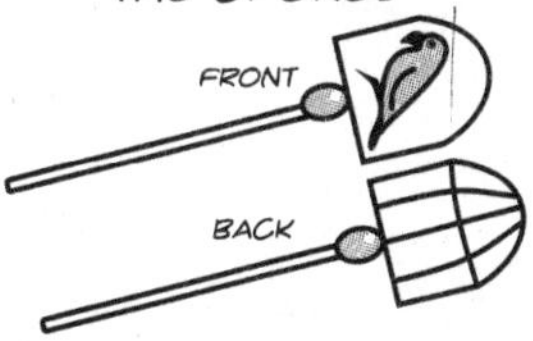

4. CUT MIDDLE PART OF STRAW AND WEAVE SPOKE IN IT.

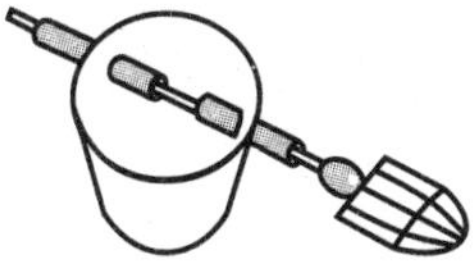

5. MAKE A HOLE IN THE BASE. TIE A THREAD TO THE SPOKE AND WEAVE IT THROUGH THE HOLE.

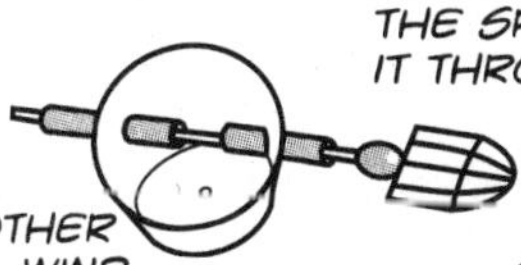

6. TIE A BEAD ON THE OTHER END OF THE THREAD. WIND IT ON THE SPOKE.

7. PULL AND RELEASE THREAD TO MAKE THE CARD SPIN. THE BIRD WILL APPEAR TO BE INSIDE THE CAGE.

CUP HELICOPTER

CUTTER

TWO STYROFOAM CUPS

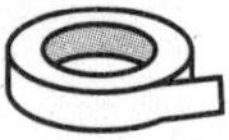

DOUBLE-SIDED TAPE OR GLUE

1. REMOVE THE BASE OF ONE CUP.

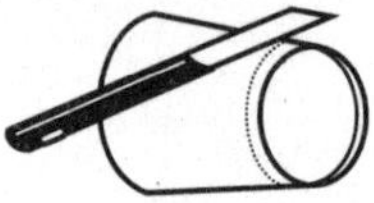

2. THEN CUT IT IN QUARTERS TO MAKE FOUR SIMILAR PETALS.

3. CUT THE RIM OF THE OTHER CUP. ITS BASE SHOULD BE FLAT.

4. STICK DOUBLE TAPE ON ITS BASE AND FIX FOUR PETALS.

5. TWIST PETALS TO MAKE BLADES.

6. DECORATE AND DROP THE CUP FROM A HEIGHT. THE CUP HELICOPTER WILL COME DOWN SPINNING.

THE CURVED BLADES OF THE FALLING HELICOPTER MAKE IT SPIN.

IRRIGATION
LADLE

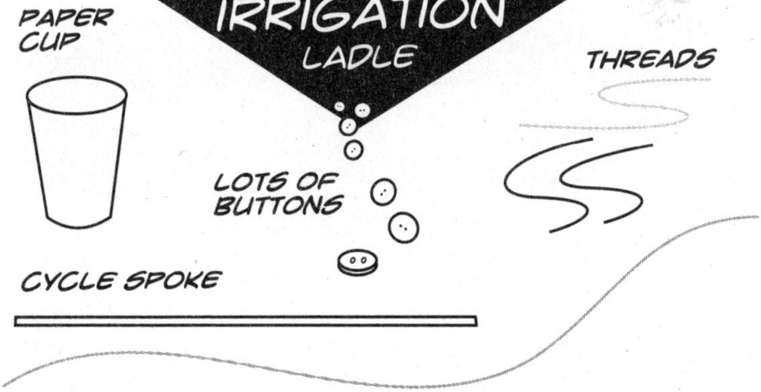

1. TIE TWO SHORT THREADS ON THE RIM OF A CUP.

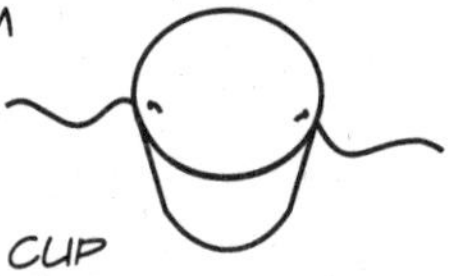

2. ALSO TIE TWO LONG THREADS NEAR THE BASE.

3. HANG THE CUP FROM A CYCLE SPOKE AS SHOWN.

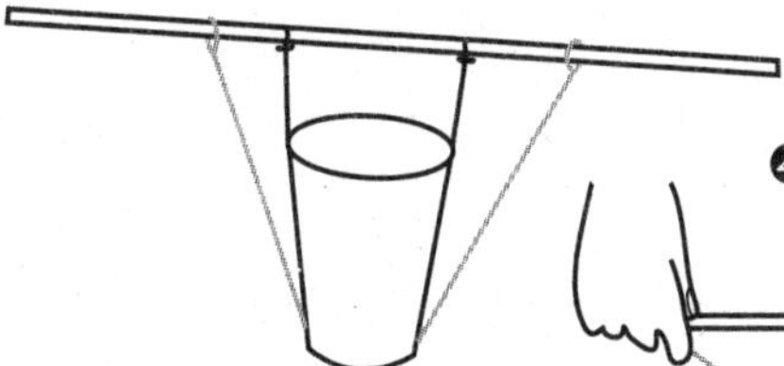

4. FILL THE CUP WITH BUTTONS.

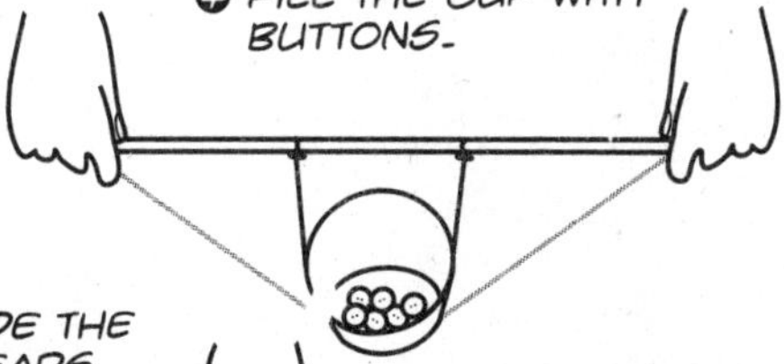

5. AS YOU SLIDE THE OUTER THREADS APART...

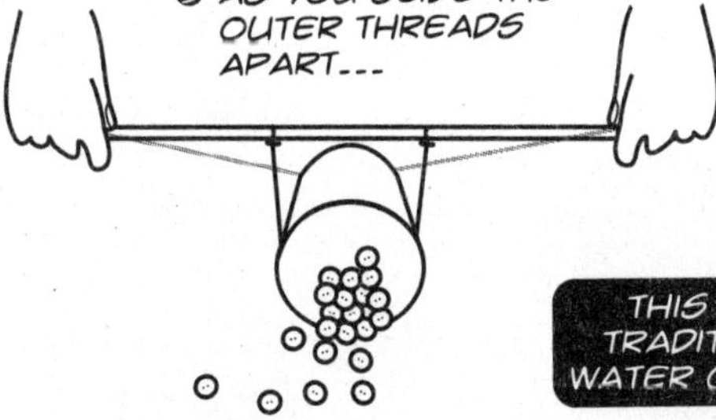

...SURPRISINGLY, THE CUP WILL TILT AND UNLOAD THE BUTTONS.

THIS TECHNIQUE WAS TRADITIONALLY USED TO WATER CROPS AND FIELDS.

BOTTLE BAG

1. CUT A BOTTLE 5 CM FROM THE TOP.

YOU WILL NEED ONLY THE TOP PART WITH THE LID.

2. FILL A THIN PLASTIC BAG WITH GOODIES.

3. WEAVE THE MOUTH OF THE BAG THROUGH THE BOTTLE.

4. FLARE THE MOUTH OF THE BAG.

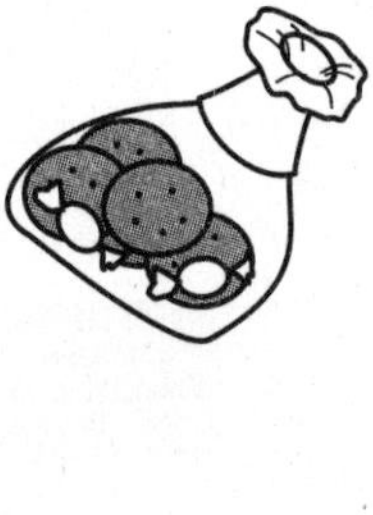

5. SCREW ON THE LID TO SEAL THE BAG. OPEN WHEN YOU WANT A TREAT.

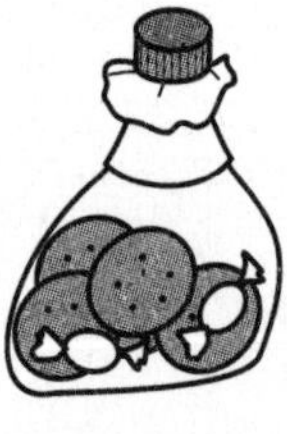

UP DOWN BUNNY

1. BEND ONE END OF A THIN STRAW...

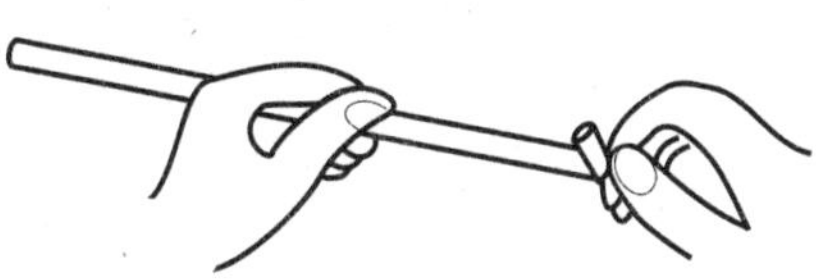

2. ... AND SEAL IT WITH TAPE.

3. STICK TWO BUNNIES BACK-TO-BACK ON THE SEALED END.

4. MAKE A HOLE IN THE LID AND GLUE A PIECE OF FAT STRAW.

5. PLACE BUNNY STRAW IN THE LID AND INSERT A PIN AS A STOPPER.

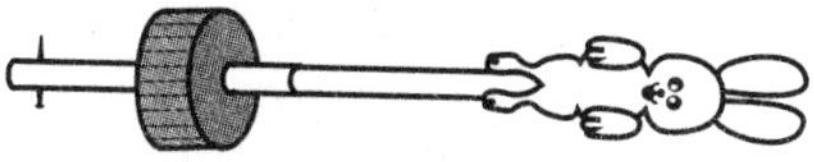

6. PLACE PIN END IN BOTTLE. THEN SCREW THE LID ON.

7. PRESS BOTTLE TO MAKE BUNNY JUMP. ON RELEASING PRESSURE, THE BUNNY WILL COME DOWN.

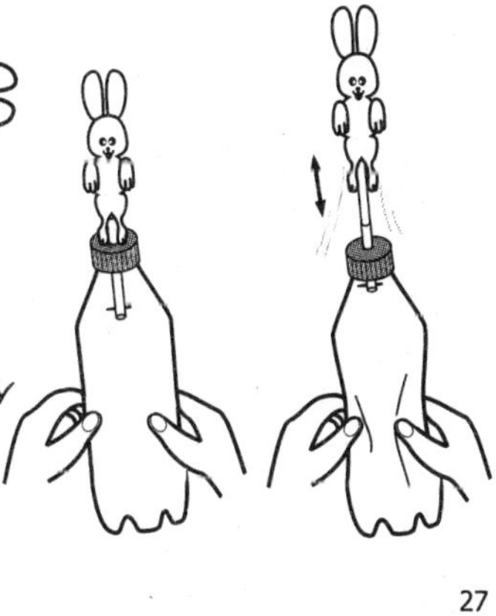

ALUMINIUM CAN BOWL

ALUMINIUM CAN

SCISSORS

❶ CUT THE TOP OF A CAN.

❷ THEN CUT LONG THIN STRIPS ALONG ITS HEIGHT.

❸ BEND ALL THE PETALS OUTWARDS, AS SHOWN.

THE PETALS WILL LOOK LIKE THE SUN'S RAYS.

❹ FOLD EACH PETAL TO TOUCH THE CAN'S RIM.

❺ KEEP FOLDING AND TUCK IN THE LAST STRIP TO MAKE A BEAUTIFUL BOWL.

KEEP SMALL TRINKETS IN THIS BOWL.

TETRA PURSE

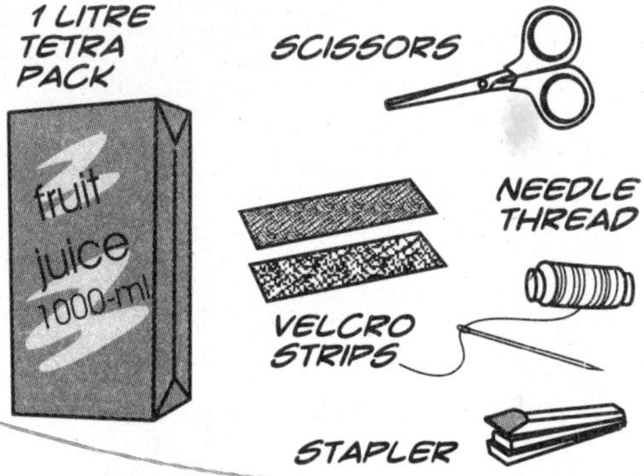

1. OPEN ALL TRIANGULAR FLAPS OF THE TETRA PACK.

2. FLATTEN IT.

3. CUT ITS TOP AND BOTTOM.

4. CUT FLAP AS SHOWN.

5. FOLD THICKNESS INWARDS.

6. FOLD IN HALF.

7. STAPLE INNER LAYERS SO THAT IT DOES NOT OPEN.

8. SEW VELCRO STRIPS TO OPEN AND CLOSE PURSE.

FIDO-DIDO CLOWN

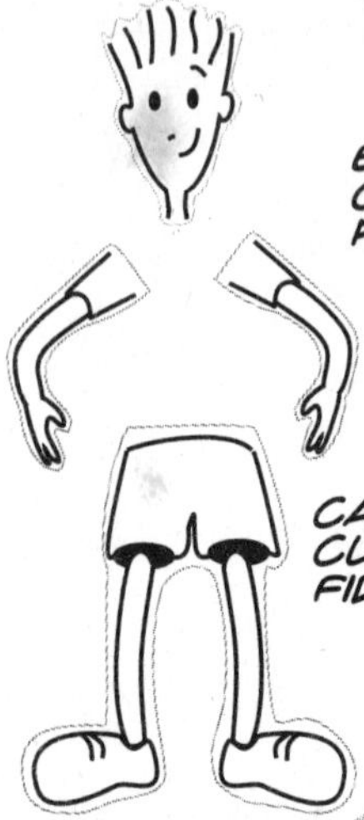

CARD SHEET CUT-OUTS OF FIDO-DIDO

EMPTY CARD PACK

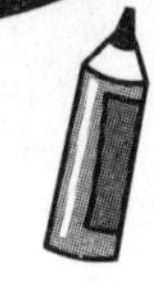

GLUE

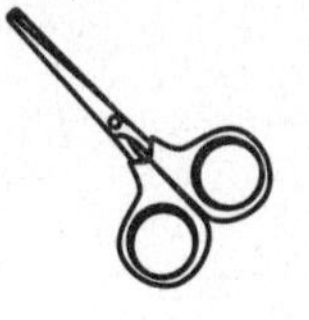

SCISSORS

1. CUT TOP AND BOTTOM FLAPS FROM A CARD PACK.

2. CUT 1.5 CM ALONG FOUR CORNERS.

3. OPEN ALL FOUR FLAPS. CUT AND SHORTEN LONG FLAPS AS SHOWN.

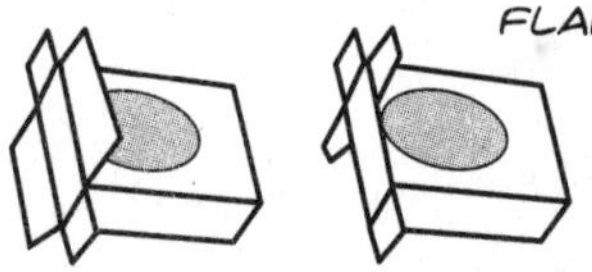

4. APPLY GLUE AND STICK CUT-OUTS OF HEAD, HANDS AND LEGS ON FLAPS.

5. PRESS AND MOVE THE BOX TO MAKE FIDO-DIDO DANCE.

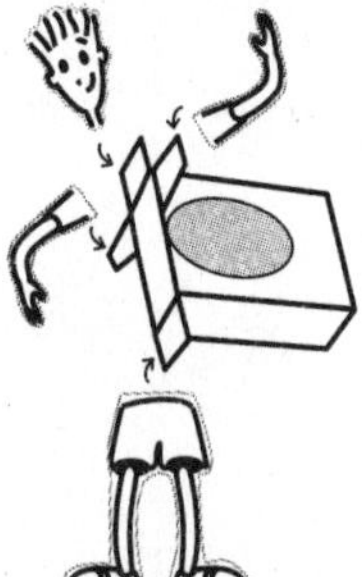

ON PRESSING, THE RECTANGULAR BOX BECOMES A PARALLELOGRAM. THIS MAKES FIDO-DIDO DANCE.

PAPER CUP PUPPET
PAPER CUP
SKETCH PENS
SCISSORS
1 DRAW RABBIT EARS AND FACE ON A PAPER CUP.
2 DRAW MIDLINE ON BOTTOM AS SHOWN.
3 CUT TO MAKE THE RABBIT'S FACE.
4 FOLD ON THE DOTTED LINE.
5 PRESS AND RELEASE FROM BEHIND TO MAKE THE PUPPET TALK.
COLOUR, DECORATE AND MAKE DIFFERENT PUPPETS.

BUTTERFLY IN THE BULB

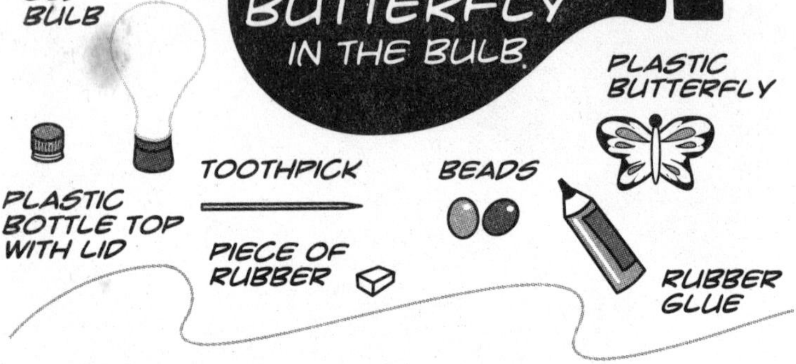

1. REMOVE THE BASE OF A FUSED BULB WITH AN ADULT'S HELP.

2. APPLY RUBBER GLUE ON THE PLASTIC BOTTLE TOP.

3. STICK THE BOTTLE TOP TO THE BULB'S MOUTH.

4. MAKE BUTTERFLY ASSEMBLY AS SHOWN. FIX IT INSIDE THE LID WITH GLUE.

5. FOLD THE WINGS AND PLACE THE BUTTERFLY IN THE BULB. SCREW THE CAP.

YOUR 'BUTTERFLY IN THE BULB' IS READY!

SPECIAL MAZE

TWO CLOTH NAPKINS

THREAD

NEEDLE

BEAD

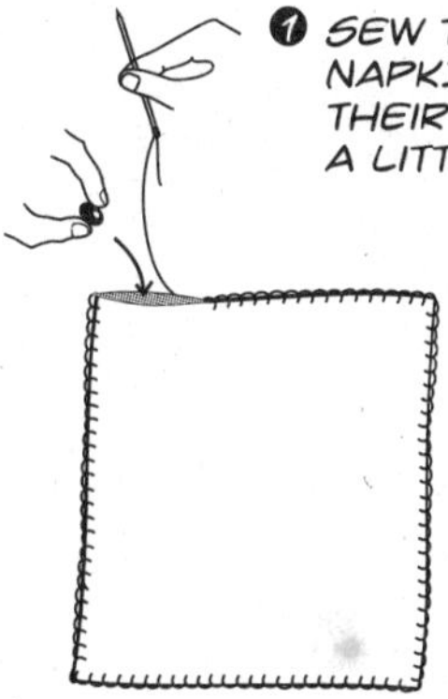

1. SEW TWO SAME-SIZED NAPKINS ALONG THEIR EDGES, LEAVING A LITTLE OPENING.
2. SLIP A BEAD IN THIS OPENING AND SEW COMPLETELY.
3. HEM DIFFERENT PATTERNS ON THE TWO NAPKINS TO MAKE A MAZE FOR THE BEAD.

4. BLINDFOLD FRIENDS AND ASK THEM TO NEGOTIATE THE BEAD THROUGH THE MAZE.

MAKE DIFFERENT MAZE PATTERNS.

THIS IS AN EXCELLENT PUZZLE FOR THE VISUALLY CHALLENGED!

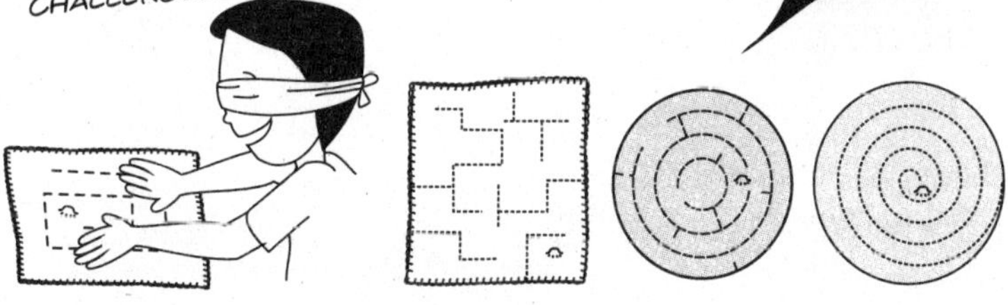

CRANKY CRANK

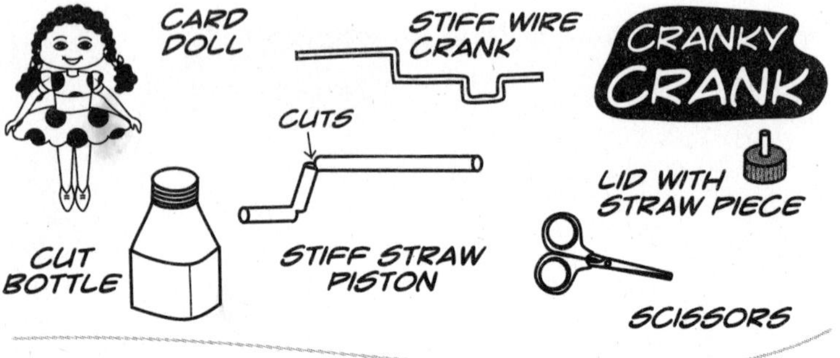

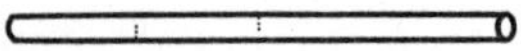

❶ MAKE TWO CUTS ON THE OPPOSITE ENDS OF A STIFF STRAW.

❷ ASSEMBLE WIRE CRANK WITH PISTON. BECAUSE OF THE TWO CUTS THE MOVING PISTON WILL BEND AND MOVE FREELY.

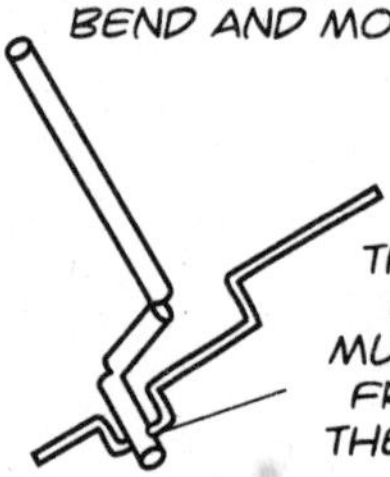

❸ MAKE TWO HOLES ON THE BOTTLE AT OPPOSITE ENDS.

❹ ASSEMBLE CRANK, PISTON IN THE BOTTLE.

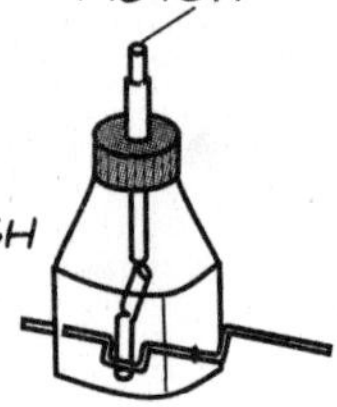

❺ INSERT PISTON THROUGH THE LID STRAW.

❻ GLUE THE DOLL TO THE PISTON STRAW.

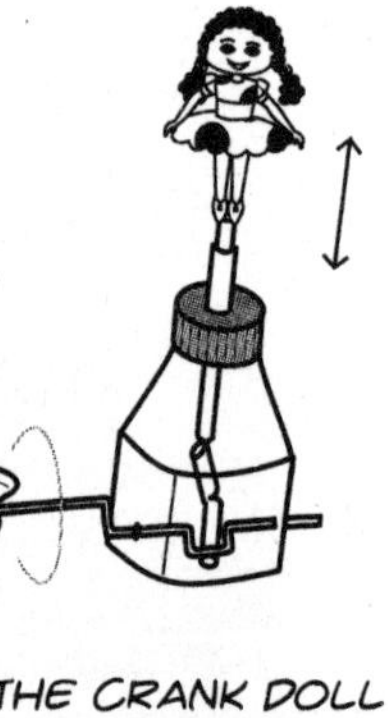

❼ ON ROTATING, THE CRANK DOLL WILL MOVE UP AND DOWN.

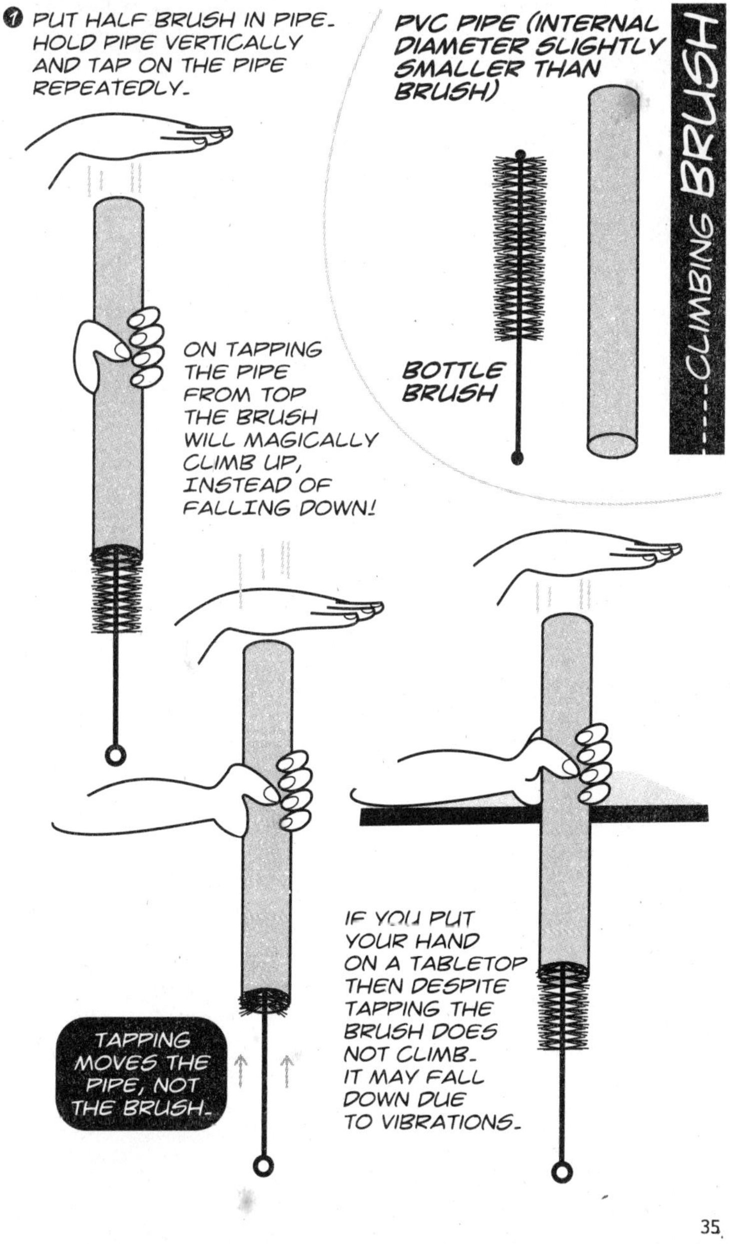
----CLIMBING BRUSH
PVC PIPE (INTERNAL DIAMETER SLIGHTLY SMALLER THAN BRUSH)
BOTTLE BRUSH
1 PUT HALF BRUSH IN PIPE. HOLD PIPE VERTICALLY AND TAP ON THE PIPE REPEATEDLY.
ON TAPPING THE PIPE FROM TOP THE BRUSH WILL MAGICALLY CLIMB UP, INSTEAD OF FALLING DOWN!
TAPPING MOVES THE PIPE, NOT THE BRUSH.
IF YOU PUT YOUR HAND ON A TABLETOP THEN DESPITE TAPPING THE BRUSH DOES NOT CLIMB. IT MAY FALL DOWN DUE TO VIBRATIONS.

BRUSH IN RUSH

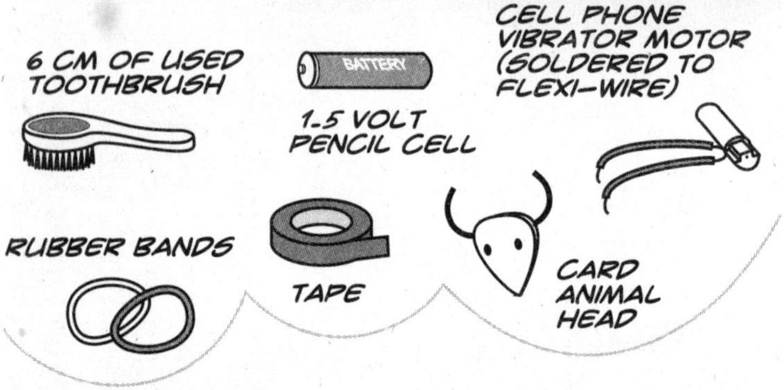

1. AFFIX VIBRATOR MOTOR TIGHTLY TO BATTERY WITH A RUBBER BAND.

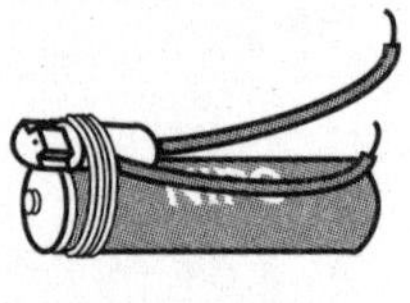

2. FIX MOTOR-VIBRATOR ASSEMBLY ON THE TOOTHBRUSH WITH A RUBBER BAND.

3. TAPE WIRE ENDS TO BATTERY TERMINALS.

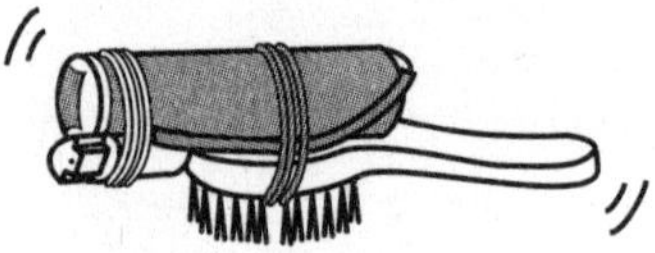

4. FIX A CARD HEAD TO MAKE IT LOOK LIKE AN ANIMAL.

THE BRUSH WILL START VIBRATING, AND THE ANIMAL WILL DANCE!

IF YOU PLACE IT ON A PLATE... IT WILL GO AROUND AND AROUND.

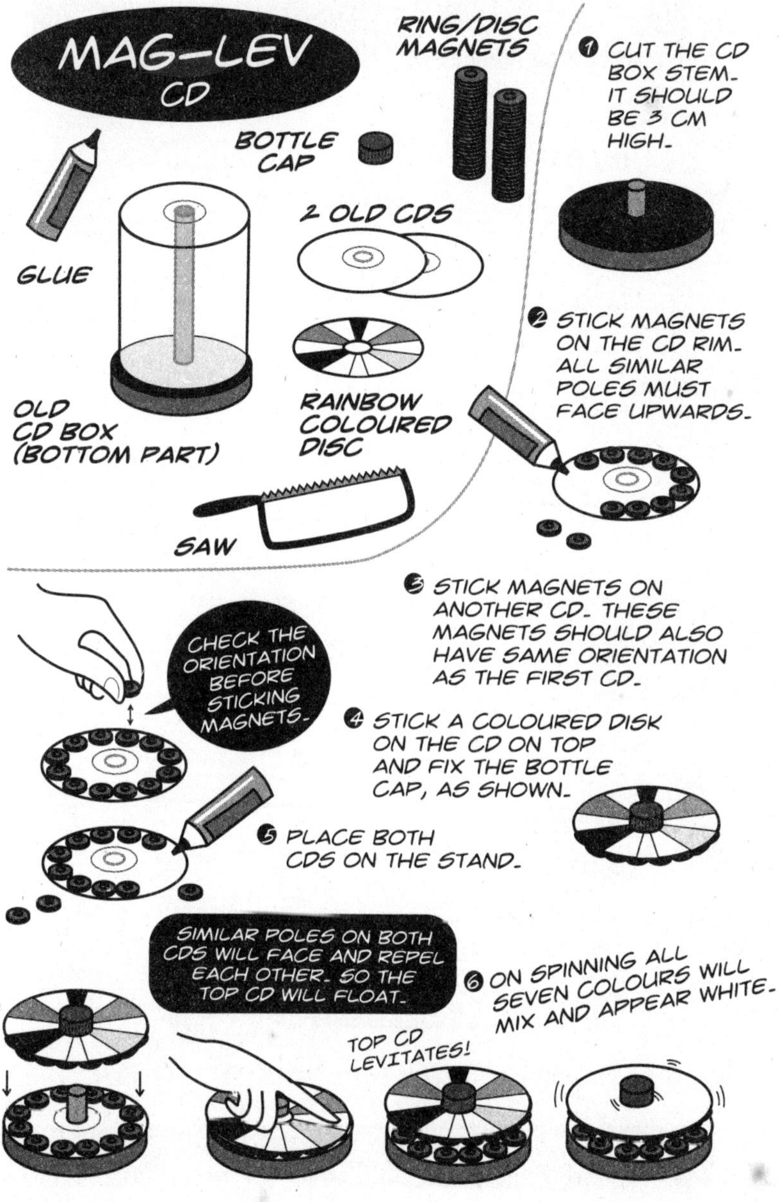

MAG-LEV CD
RING/DISC MAGNETS
BOTTLE CAP
GLUE
2 OLD CDS
OLD CD BOX (BOTTOM PART)
RAINBOW COLOURED DISC
SAW
1 CUT THE CD BOX STEM. IT SHOULD BE 3 CM HIGH.
2 STICK MAGNETS ON THE CD RIM. ALL SIMILAR POLES MUST FACE UPWARDS.
CHECK THE ORIENTATION BEFORE STICKING MAGNETS.
3 STICK MAGNETS ON ANOTHER CD. THESE MAGNETS SHOULD ALSO HAVE SAME ORIENTATION AS THE FIRST CD.
4 STICK A COLOURED DISK ON THE CD ON TOP AND FIX THE BOTTLE CAP, AS SHOWN.
5 PLACE BOTH CDS ON THE STAND.
SIMILAR POLES ON BOTH CDS WILL FACE AND REPEL EACH OTHER. SO THE TOP CD WILL FLOAT.
6 ON SPINNING ALL SEVEN COLOURS WILL MIX AND APPEAR WHITE.
TOP CD LEVITATES!

MAGNETIC SLOW SLIDE

1. HOLD THE ALUMINIUM PLATE AT A SLANT.

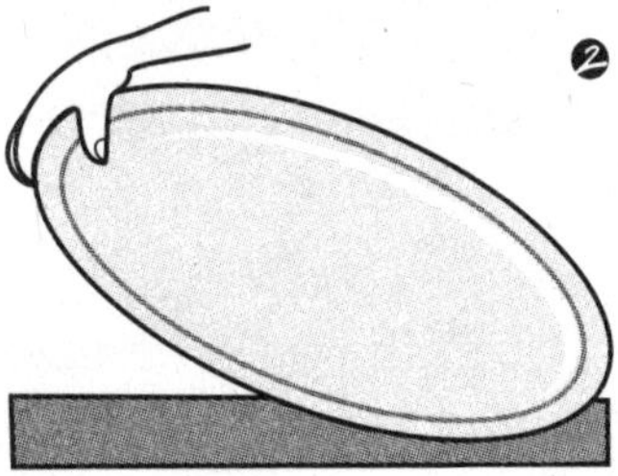

2. PLACE THE NEODYMIUM MAGNET ON THE PLATE. BECAUSE OF EDDY CURRENTS IT WILL SLIDE SLOWLY.

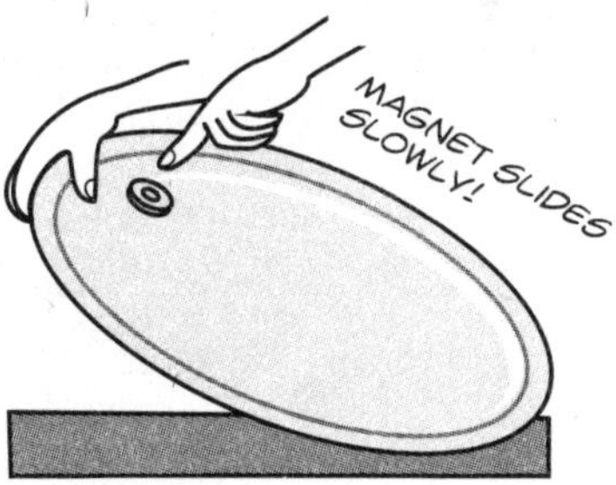

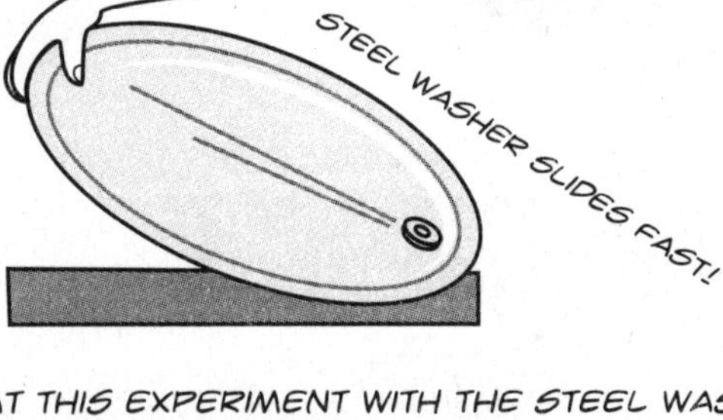

- REPEAT THIS EXPERIMENT WITH THE STEEL WASHER.

AS THERE ARE NO EDDY CURRENTS, THE STEEL WASHER WILL SLIDE FAST ON THE ALUMINIUM PLATE.

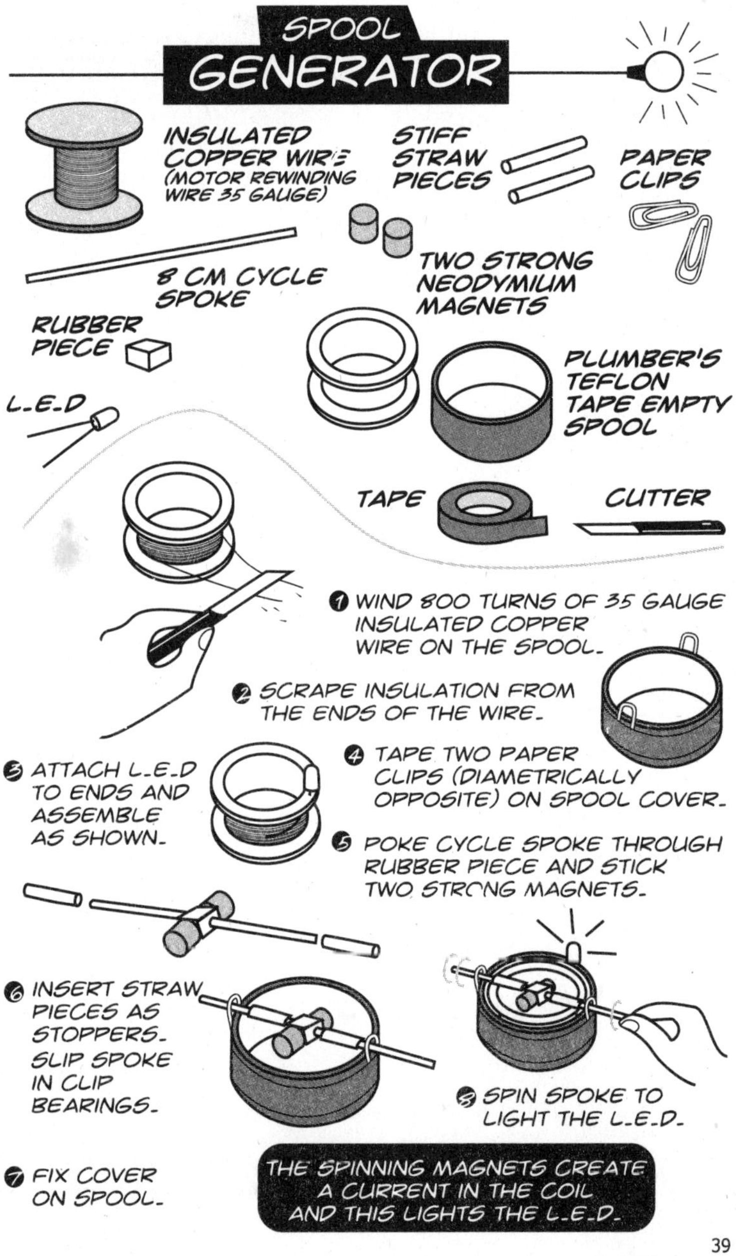
SPOOL
GENERATOR
INSULATED COPPER WIRE (MOTOR REWINDING WIRE 35 GAUGE)
STIFF STRAW PIECES
PAPER CLIPS
8 CM CYCLE SPOKE
TWO STRONG NEODYMIUM MAGNETS
RUBBER PIECE
PLUMBER'S TEFLON TAPE EMPTY SPOOL
L.E.D
TAPE
CUTTER
1 WIND 800 TURNS OF 35 GAUGE INSULATED COPPER WIRE ON THE SPOOL.
2 SCRAPE INSULATION FROM THE ENDS OF THE WIRE.
3 ATTACH L.E.D TO ENDS AND ASSEMBLE AS SHOWN.
4 TAPE TWO PAPER CLIPS (DIAMETRICALLY OPPOSITE) ON SPOOL COVER.
5 POKE CYCLE SPOKE THROUGH RUBBER PIECE AND STICK TWO STRONG MAGNETS.
6 INSERT STRAW PIECES AS STOPPERS. SLIP SPOKE IN CLIP BEARINGS.
7 FIX COVER ON SPOOL.
8 SPIN SPOKE TO LIGHT THE L.E.D.
THE SPINNING MAGNETS CREATE A CURRENT IN THE COIL AND THIS LIGHTS THE L.E.D.

PENTAGON

1. TAKE AN A-4 SHEET.

2. FOLD IN QUARTER TO LOCATE ITS CENTRE.

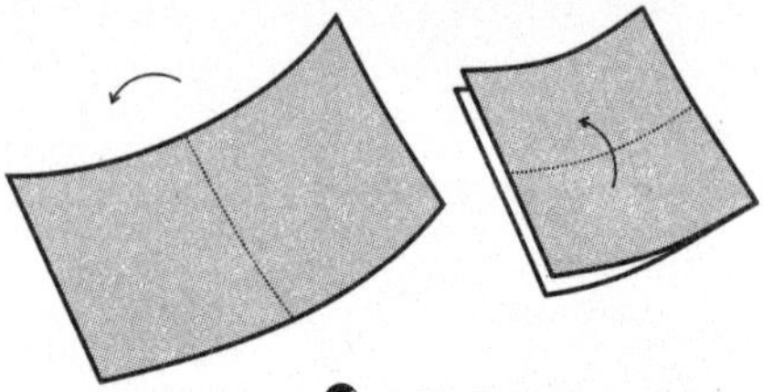

3. FOLD ALL FOUR CORNERS TO CENTRE.

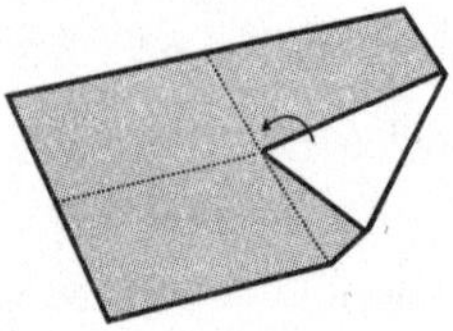

4. FOLD THE MODEL IN HALF.

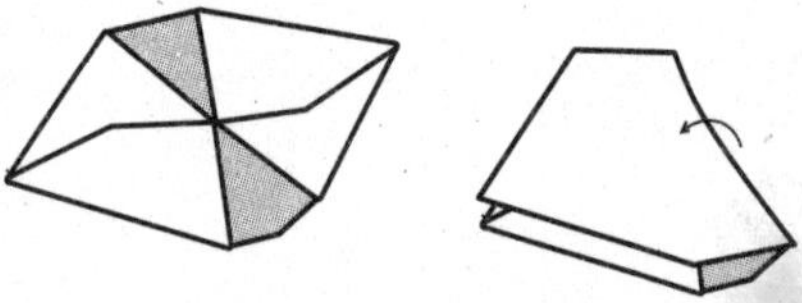

5. FOLD POINT 'A' TO MIDLINE, SO THAT LINE AC IS PARALLEL TO THE BASE.

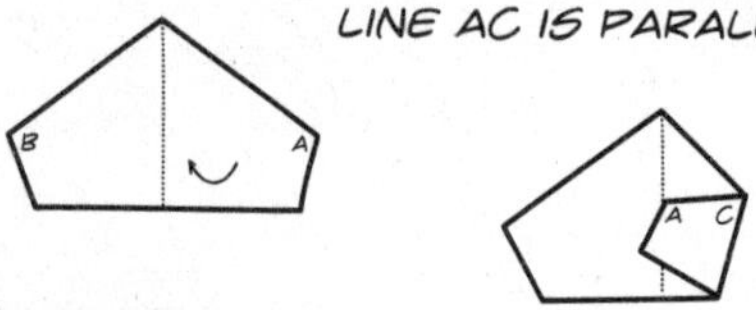

6. FOLD BOTH SIDES.

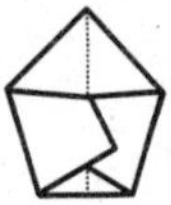

7. OPEN THE PENTAGON.

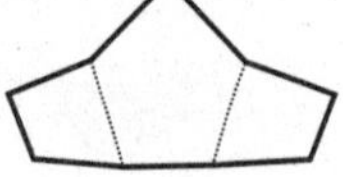

8. REVERSE FOLD IT.

9. TUCK RIGHT SIDE IN.

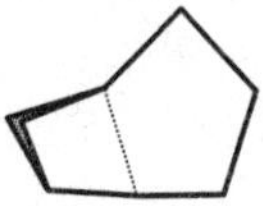

10. OPEN FLAP AS SHOWN.

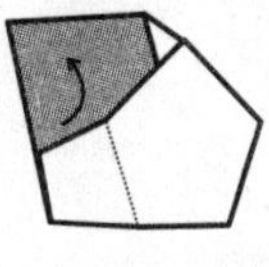

11. REVERSE FOLD IT.

12. TUCK THE FLAP INSIDE...

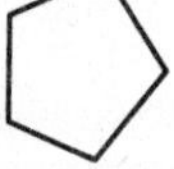

...TO MAKE A BEAUTIFUL PENTAGON!

PENTAGON BIRDS

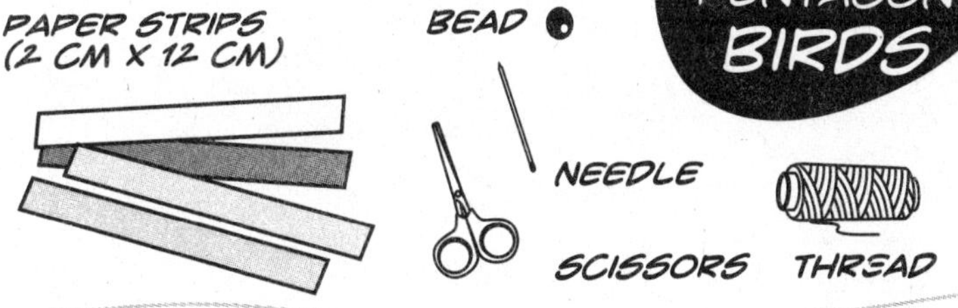

1. HOLD THE TWO ENDS OF A LONG PAPER STRIP AND TIE A SIMPLE KNOT.

2. GENTLY PULL THE ENDS AND YOU WILL BE SURPRISED TO SEE A PENTAGONAL KNOT IN THE MIDDLE.

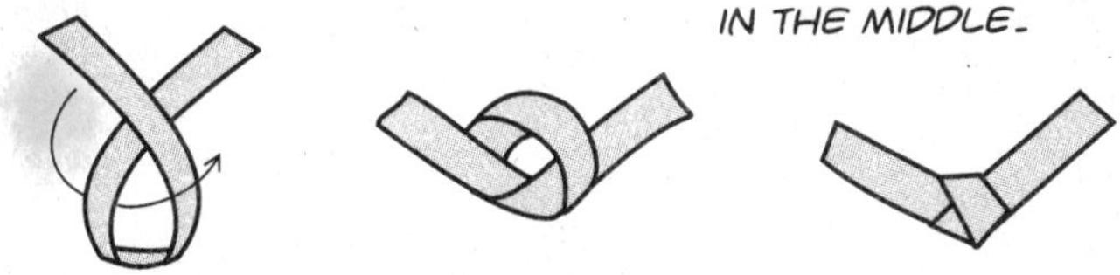

3. MARK A BEAK AND TAIL AS SHOWN.

4. CUT ALONG THE MARKED LINES.

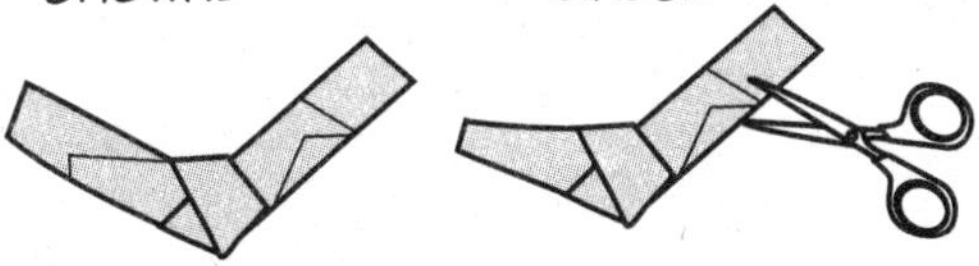

5. DRAW AN EYE AND THE PENTAGON BIRD IS READY.

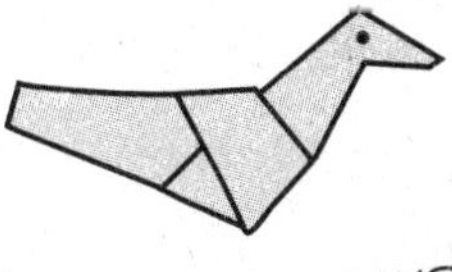

MAKE MANY COLOURFUL BIRDS. WEAVE THEM ALONG A THREAD TO MAKE A PRETTY WALL HANGING.

ENVELOPE TETRAHEDRON

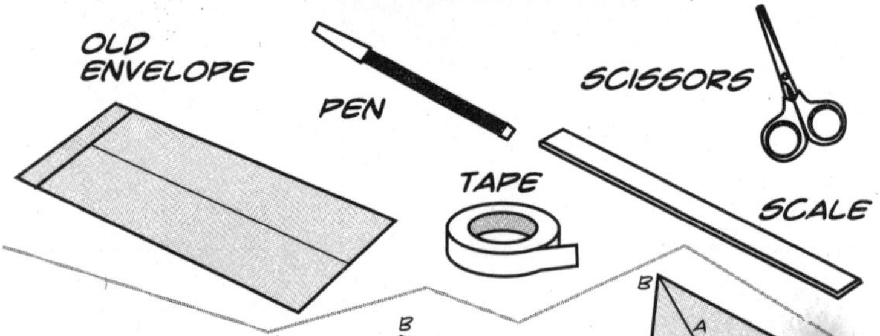

1. FOLD THE MIDLINE OF AN ENVELOPE ALONG ITS LENGTH.

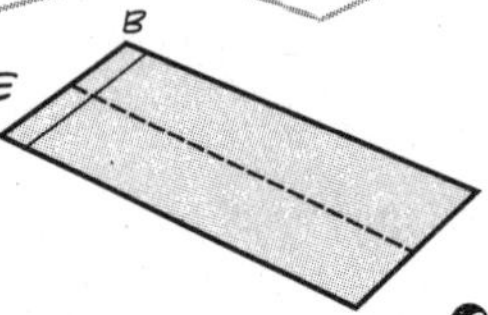

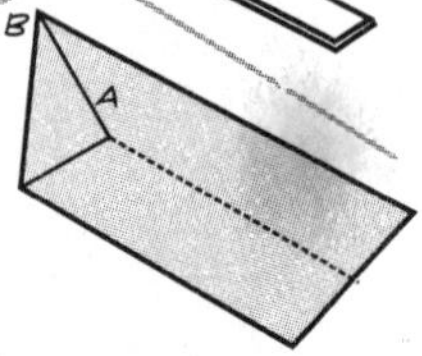

2. FOLD POINT 'A' TO MIDLINE THROUGH 'B'.

3. MARK THE LINE AND CUT...

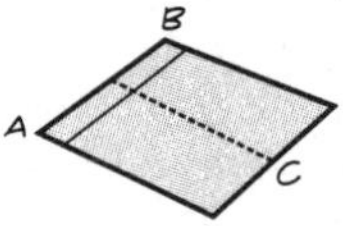

...TO MAKE A RECTANGLE.

4. DRAW LINES CA AND CB...

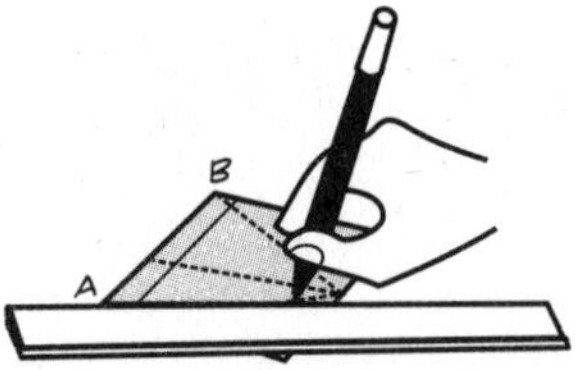

5. ... AND CREASE ALONG THEM.

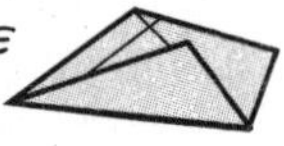

6. THEN OPEN THE MOUTH AND TAPE THE OPEN ENDS TO MAKE A BEAUTIFUL TETRAHEDRON!

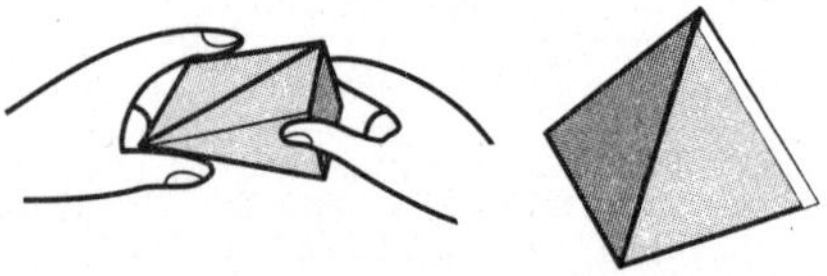

POSTCARD GARLAND

❶ FOLD A POSTCARD IN HALF ALONG ITS LENGTH.

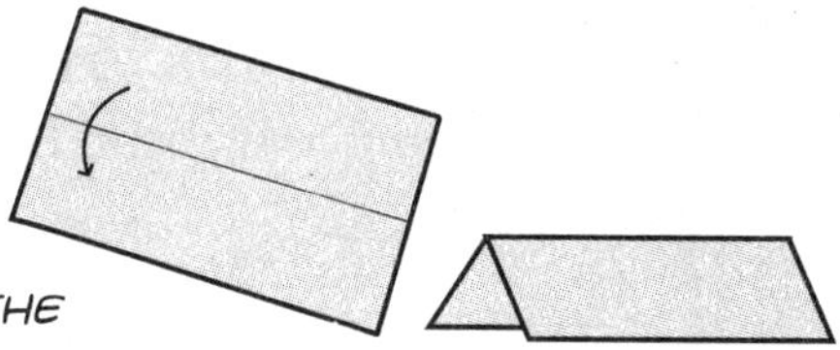

❷ DRAW LINES ALONG THE WIDTH AS SHOWN.

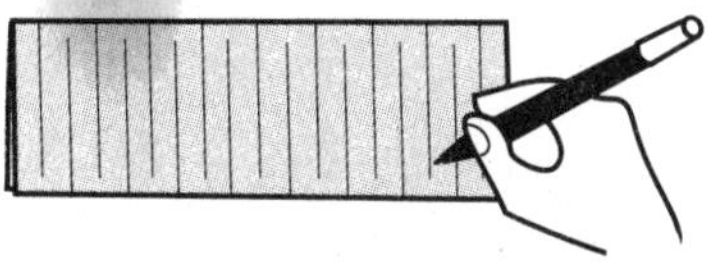

❸ CUT ALONG THE LINES FROM BOTH ENDS.

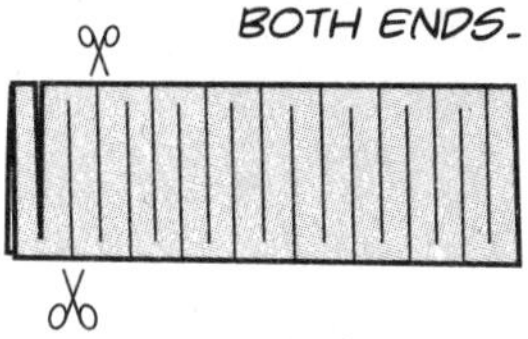

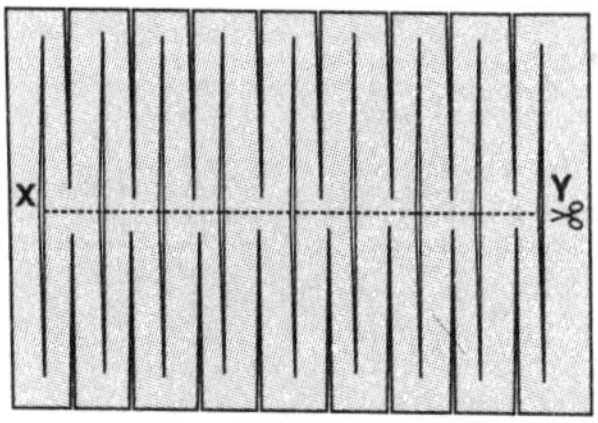

❹ OPEN THE POSTCARD AND CUT FROM POINT X TO Y TO GET A GARLAND.

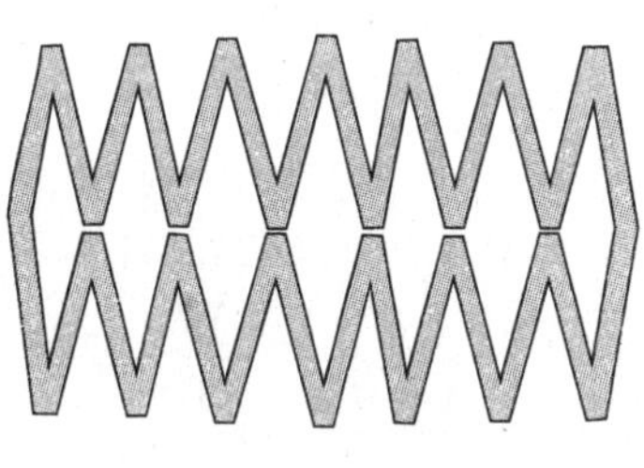

❺ YOU CAN WEAR THIS LARGE GARLAND.

HOPPING BIRD

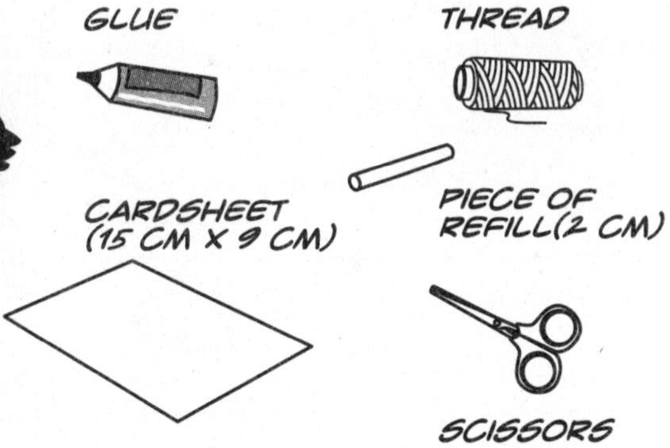

1. DRAW AND CUT THIS DOUBLE BIRD ON A THICK CARDSHEET.

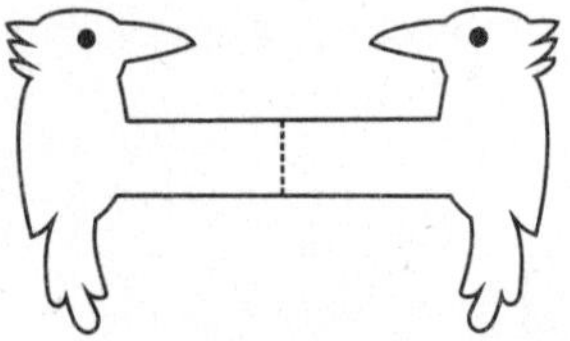

2. STICK A 2 CM LONG, EMPTY BALL PEN REFILL PIECE VERTICALLY IN THE MIDDLE.

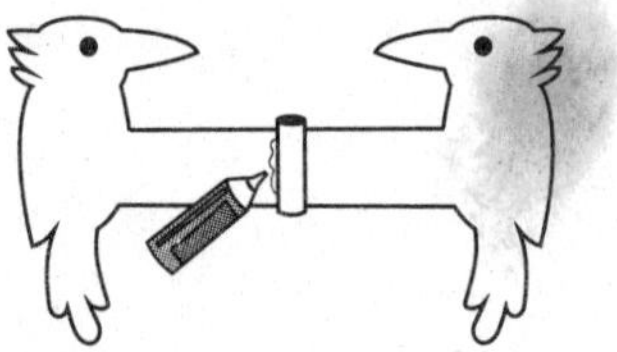

3. APPLY GLUE, DOUBLE FOLD AND STICK THE BIRD. COLOUR THE BIRD.

4. WEAVE A THREAD IN THE REFILL AND TIE TWO BEADS ON THE ENDS OF THE THREAD.

5. ON HOLDING THE THREAD TIGHT, THE BIRD WILL COME DOWN IN SHORT JERKS!

MORE WEIGHT ON ONE SIDE AND THE FRICTION OF THE THREAD MAKE THE BIRD FALL IN SHORT JERKS.

ROBOTIC FINGER

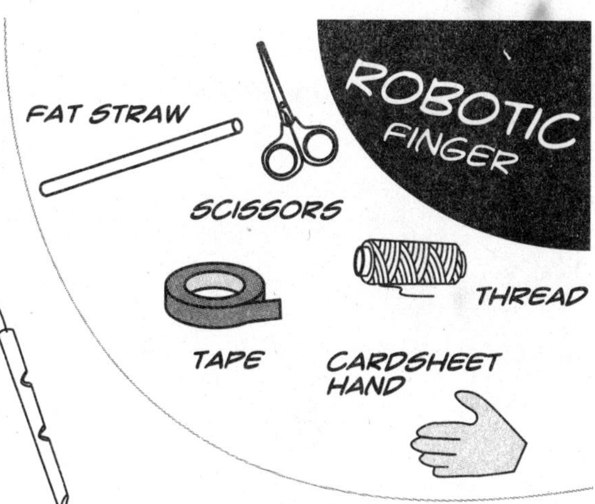

1. CUT FOUR 'V'-SHAPED NOTCHES IN A FAT PLASTIC STRAW.

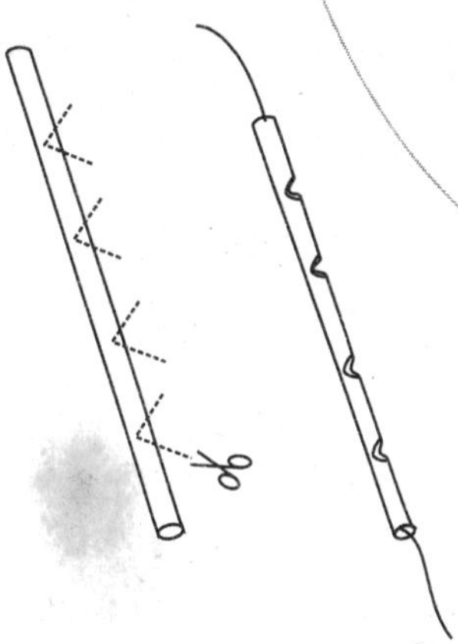

2. WEAVE THIN THREAD THROUGH THE STRAW.

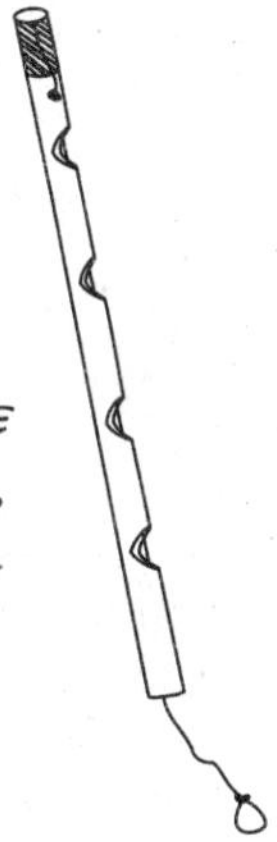

3. TAPE ONE END OF THE THREAD TO THE TOP END OF THE STRAW. TIE A LOOP AT THE OTHER END.

4. HOLD THE STRAW WITH ONE HAND AND PULL THE LOOP WITH THE OTHER TO MAKE THE ROBOTIC FINGER CURL. RELEASE BEAD TO STRAIGHTEN THE STRAW.

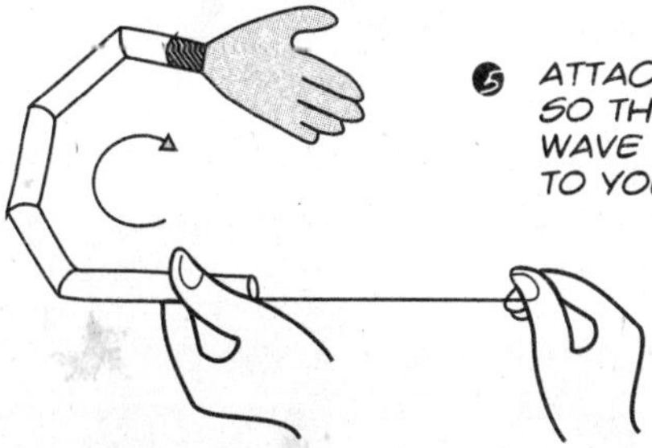

5. ATTACH A CARD HAND SO THAT YOU CAN WAVE A GOOD-BYE TO YOUR FRIENDS.

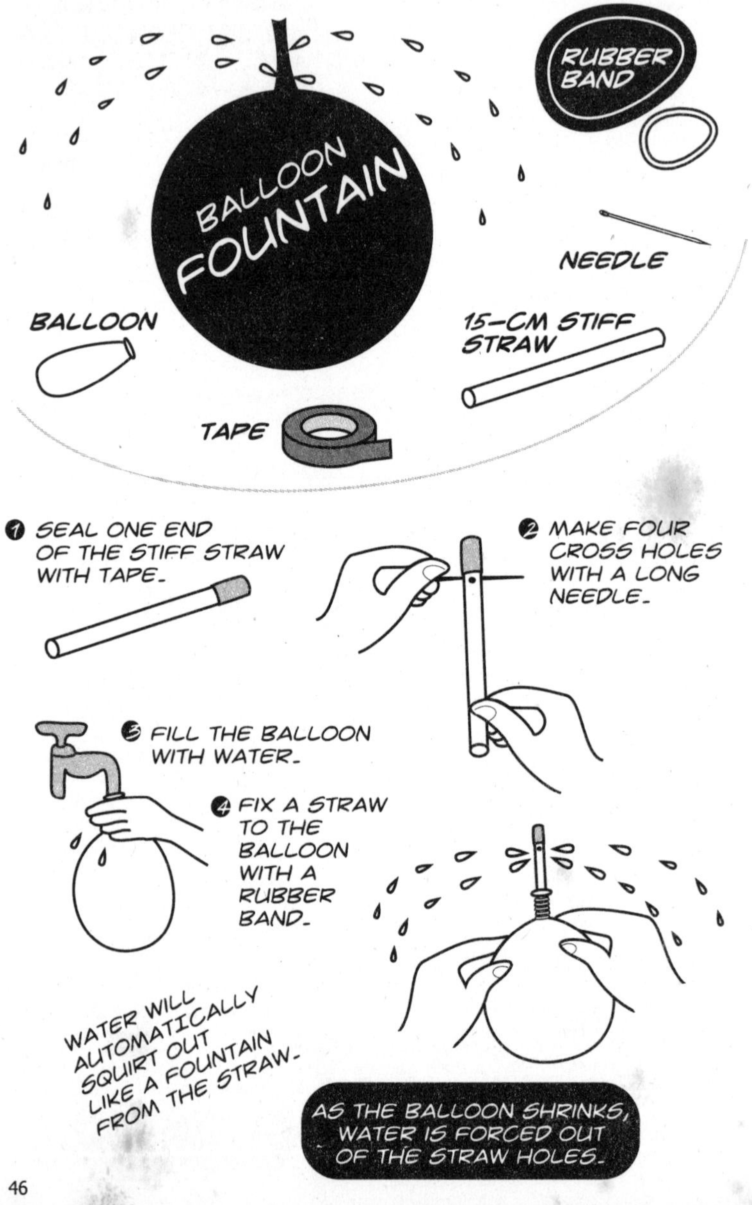

BALLOON FOUNTAIN
RUBBER BAND
NEEDLE
BALLOON
15-CM STIFF STRAW
TAPE
1 SEAL ONE END OF THE STIFF STRAW WITH TAPE.
2 MAKE FOUR CROSS HOLES WITH A LONG NEEDLE.
3 FILL THE BALLOON WITH WATER.
4 FIX A STRAW TO THE BALLOON WITH A RUBBER BAND.
WATER WILL AUTOMATICALLY SQUIRT OUT LIKE A FOUNTAIN FROM THE STRAW.
AS THE BALLOON SHRINKS, WATER IS FORCED OUT OF THE STRAW HOLES.

SUBMARINE

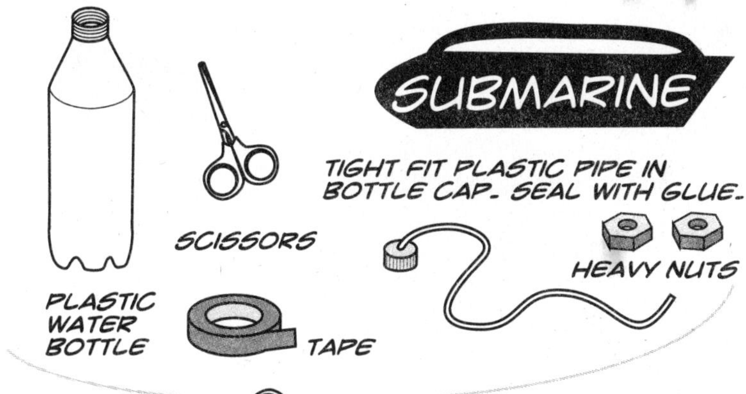

1. POKE THREE HOLES IN A LINE WITH SCISSORS.
2. TAPE TWO HEAVY NUTS BETWEEN THE HOLES.
3. TIGHTEN THE BOTTLE LID.

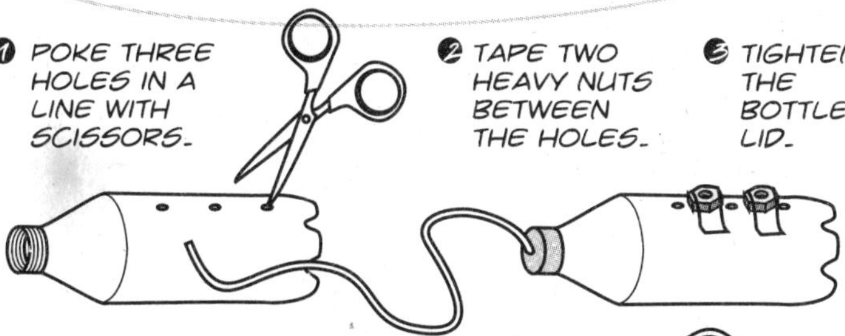

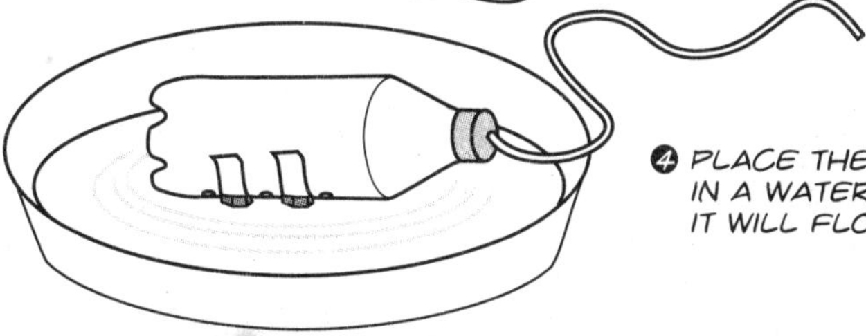

4. PLACE THE BOTTLE IN A WATER TUB. IT WILL FLOAT.

5. NOW SUCK THROUGH THE TUBE. AS YOU SUCK, WATER WILL FILL THE BOTTLE MAKING IT HEAVY AND IT WILL SLOWLY SINK.

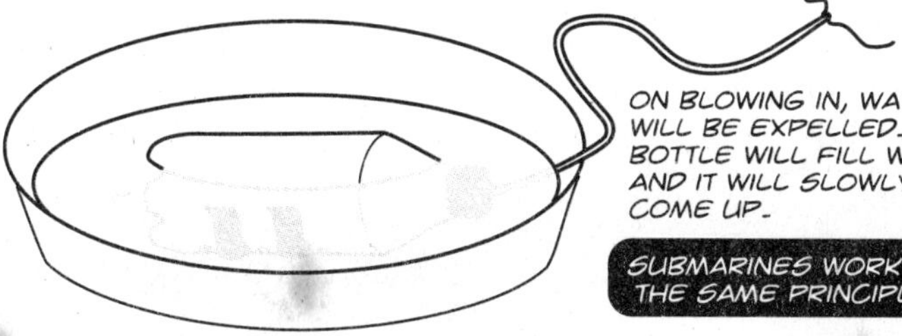

ON BLOWING IN, WATER WILL BE EXPELLED. THE BOTTLE WILL FILL WITH AIR AND IT WILL SLOWLY COME UP.

SUBMARINES WORK ON THE SAME PRINCIPLE.

STRAW SPRAY

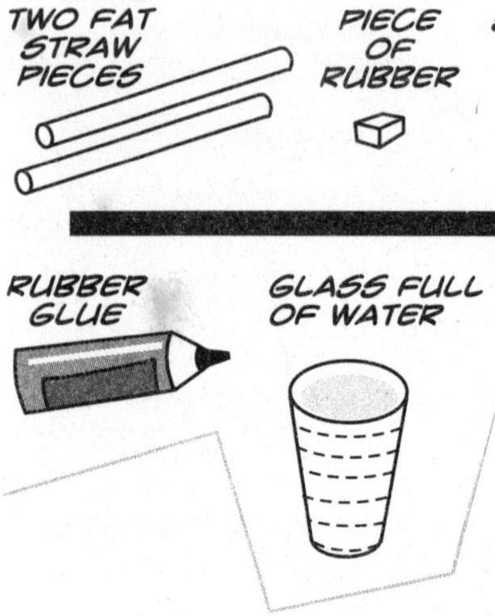

1. JOIN TWO FAT STRAWS AT 90-DEGREES TO MAKE A SPRAY PIPE.

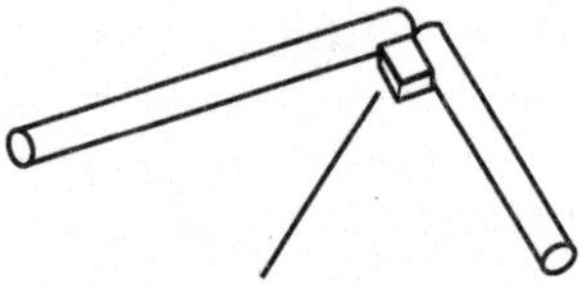

2. STICK A PIECE OF RUBBER FOR SUPPORT. THIS WILL KEEP THE STRAWS AT RIGHT ANGLES.

3. DIP ONE END IN WATER AND BLOW. WATER SPRAY WILL COME OUT LIKE A MIST!

USE A FAT STRAW TO SPRAY STYROFOAM BALLS INSTEAD OF WATER.

MEOW MEOW...

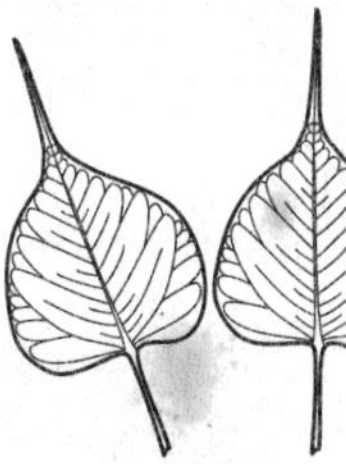

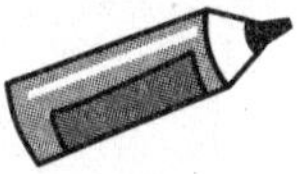

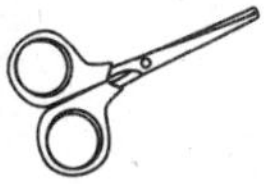

RUBBER GLUE

SCISSORS

TWO PEEPAL (FICUS RELIGIOSA) LEAVES

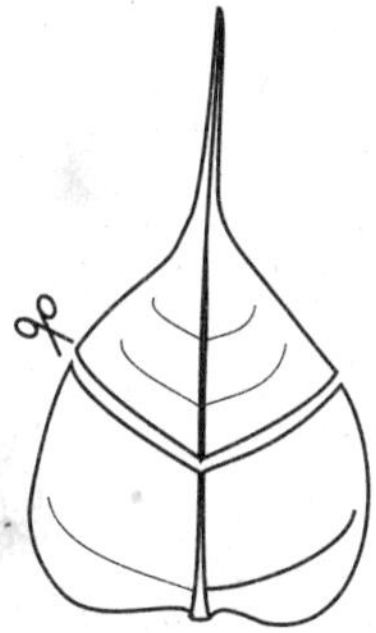

1. MAKE TWO SLANT CUTS ON THE FIRST HEART SHAPED LEAF TO MAKE THE CAT'S FACE.

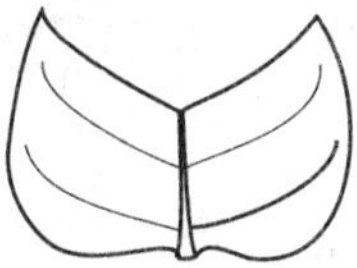

2. CUT THE SECOND LEAF ALONG THE MIDRIB. HALF THE LEAF ALONG WITH ITS STEM WILL MAKE THE CAT'S BODY AND THE TAIL.

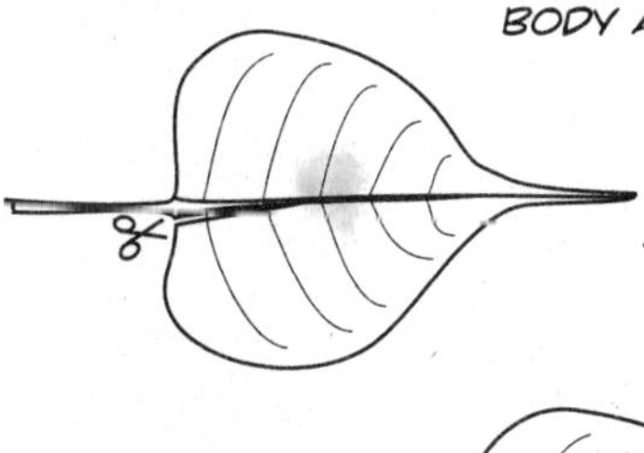

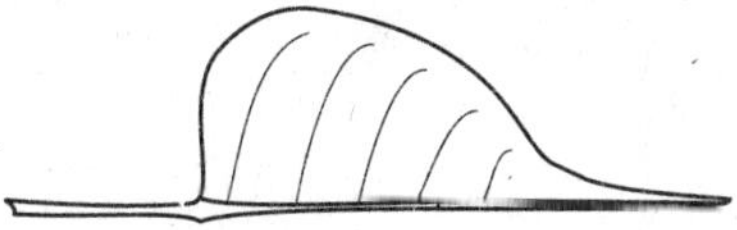

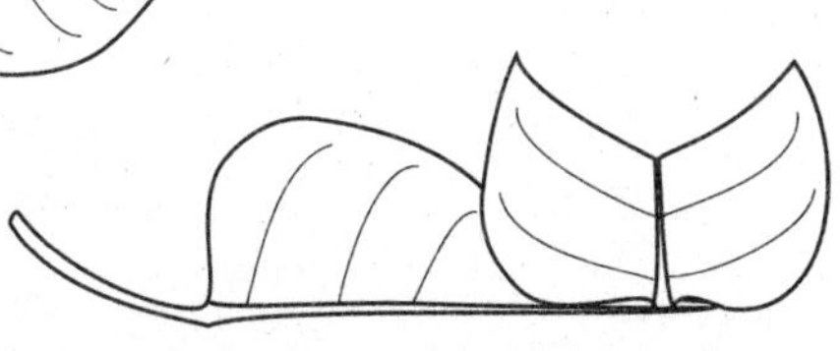

3. STICK THE TWO PIECES TO MAKE THE LEAF CAT.

ANIMAL JIGSAW

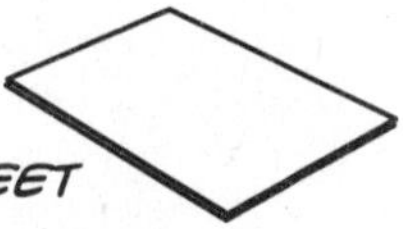

CARDSHEET

CUTTER

1. DRAW 18 ANIMALS ON A THICK CARDBOARD OR PLYWOOD. THEN CUT THEM WITH A CRAFT KNIFE OR A FRET SAW. YOU CAN STAND THESE ANIMALS INDIVIDUALLY TO MAKE A ZOO OR SNUG THEM TOGETHER INTO A JIGSAW.